W9-AXY-149

## Holly Was Devastated

And she was scared. Craig had nearly been caught in Los Angeles. How else could the FBI have known where he would be if not for David?

And that night, that shattering night, when they had almost made love, David had said, *"I can help you, Holly. If you'll just allow yourself to trust me, I swear I can help you."*

He knew, she was sure he knew. And as far as Holly was concerned, that was reason enough not to see him again. Ever.

Dear Reader:

Romance offers us all so much. It makes us "walk on sunshine." It gives us hope. It takes us out of our own lives, encouraging us to reach out to others. Janet Dailey is fond of saying that romance is a state of mind, that it could happen anywhere. Yet nowhere does romance seem to be as good as when it happens *here*.

Starting in February 1986, Silhouette Special Edition will feature the AMERICAN TRIBUTE—a tribute to America, where romance has never been so wonderful. For six consecutive months, one out of every six Special Editions will be an episode in the AMERICAN TRIBUTE, a portrait of the lives of six women, all from Oklahoma. Look for the first book, *Love's Haunting Refrain* by Ada Steward, as well as stories by other favorites—Jeanne Stephens, Gena Dalton, Elaine Camp and Renee Roszel. You'll know the AMERICAN TRIBUTE by its patriotic stripe under the Silhouette Special Edition border.

AMERICAN TRIBUTE—six women, six stories, starting in February.

AMERICAN TRIBUTE—one of the reasons Silhouette Special Edition is just that—Special.

The Editors at Silhouette Books

# LINDA
# LAEL MILLER
## State
## Secrets

*Silhouette Special Edition*

Published by Silhouette Books New York

**America's Publisher of Contemporary Romance**

For Mary Clare Kersten.
Thank you for your encouragement, your diplomacy,
and your blue pencil.

SILHOUETTE BOOKS
300 E. 42nd St., New York, N.Y. 10017

Copyright © 1985 by Linda Lael Miller

Distributed by Pocket Books

All rights reserved, including the right to reproduce
this book or portions thereof in any form whatsoever.
For information address Silhouette Books,
300 E. 42nd St., New York, N.Y. 10017

ISBN: 0-373-09277-6

First Silhouette Books printing December 1985

10 9 8 7 6 5 4 3 2 1

All the characters in this book are fictitious. Any
resemblance to actual persons, living or dead, is purely
coincidental.

SILHOUETTE, SILHOUETTE SPECIAL EDITION and colophon are
registered trademarks of the publisher.

America's Publisher of Contemporary Romance

Printed in the U.S.A.

**Books by Linda Lael Miller**

Silhouette Intimate Moments

*Snowflakes on the Sea #59*
*Part of the Bargain #87*

Silhouette Special Edition

*State Secrets #277*

# LINDA LAEL MILLER

lives with her characters, sharing their dreams, joys and
sorrows. They become real to her, and often surprise her
with their actions. When the book is done, the parting is
bearable only because she knows new people are crowding
around her typewriter, eager to tell their stories.

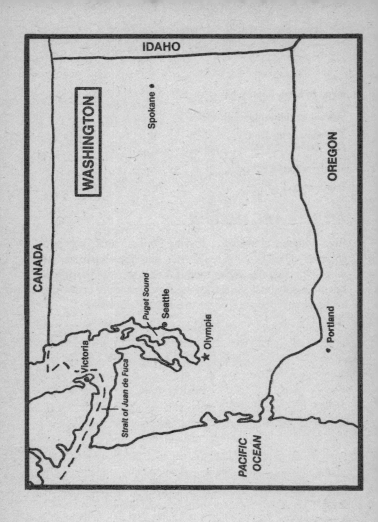

## Chapter One

The tall man ran one hand through his dark hair and shifted uncomfortably in his seat. Despite the heavy woolen overcoat he wore, he was still cold. Swift indigo eyes scanned the first page of the dossier. "So what, Walt?" David Goddard bit out, frowning. "She's the president-elect's third cousin. Since when do third cousins qualify for Secret Service protection?"

Walt Zigman made a contemptuous, impatient sound. Apparently, this assignment wasn't exactly dear to his crusty old heart. "It isn't protection, Goddard," he snarled. "Remember that. This is a surveillance project."

David sat back in his chair, drawing his right ankle up to rest on his left knee. "Surveillance," he muttered, suppressing an unprofessional urge to fling the file on Holly Llewellyn back into the mess that littered Walt's desk. "That isn't our—"

"I know, Goddard," Walt interrupted, falling into his own chair and reaching into one ink-stained shirt pocket for a match to light the cigar stub that was always in his mouth. "I know. I tried to give this thing to the Bureau. I even tried the CIA. But they both threw it right back in my lap. Anything connected with the president or his family is our bailiwick—according to them."

David breathed a swearword. He was tired and he could still feel the bite of the crisp November wind outside. He wanted to get out of Washington and have Thanksgiving dinner in Arlington with his sister, Chris, and her family. He wanted to spoil her kids and lounge in front of her fireplace. "Okay, Walt. So Ms. Llewellyn is our problem. Why am I the lucky one?"

Walt chortled. "Born under the right star, I guess. Come on, Goddard, how bad can it be? You spend a few weeks—maybe a few months—in Spokane. You get the lady to like you. And you make damned sure she's really what she claims to be, and not a courier for that brother of hers."

David had the beginnings of a headache. He opened the dossier again, skimming the rundown on Holly Llewellyn. Twenty-seven years old. Blonde. Blue-eyed. Five feet, seven inches tall. A one hundred twenty-three pound pain. "What makes you think she's running secrets? It says here she writes cookbooks."

"Chinese cookbooks," David's supervisor imparted with dramatic import.

David's mouth twisted into a wry grin. "That alone should convict her," he mocked.

"Dammit, Goddard, keep your sparkling wit to yourself. Can't you see that we've got the makings of a scandal here that would make Watergate seem insignificant?"

"A scandal?"

"Yes! How would it look if the new president's cousin turned out to be a traitor? Isn't it bad enough that her brother sold out? She could be cut from the same cloth!"

David sighed. "That's unlikely, Walt. It says here that she's written a book about Scandinavian meatballs. Good God, maybe she's spying for the Swedes!"

"Stow it."

"Or the Danes. You've got to watch those Danes, crafty little devils, one and all."

"Goddard!"

"She wrote *Fun With Tacos*, too, I see," David pressed on dryly. "Do you think she's working for the Mexicans? Holy guacamole, Batman—do you suppose they're planning to rush up here and take back Texas?"

Walt was leaning into the desk, his meaty hands braced against the edge, his cigar stub bobbing up and down in outrage. "I'm glad you think this situation is funny, Goddard, but it just so happens that the next president of the United States doesn't agree with you! This little lady happens to have a bona fide, card-carrying traitor for a brother!"

David flipped through the rest of the dossier, not so hastily this time. His headache was worse. "Craig Llewellyn," he muttered.

"You remember him, don't you, Goddard?" Walt gibed, going to stand at the barred window of his dingy little office.

Remember? David remembered, all right—how could he help it? Craig Llewellyn's defection had never made the national news, by some miracle, but every federal agent in the country knew the sordid story. "Being Llewellyn's sister doesn't make the lady a security risk, Walt," he pointed out quietly.

"Maybe not. If she wasn't related to our next president, I wouldn't be worried. If she hadn't just spent two months in mainland China, I wouldn't be worried. As it is, I'm *damned* worried."

"You'd think the opposition would have caught on to this before the election..." David speculated, thinking of the outgoing president and the no-holds-barred campaign he had conducted.

"They didn't," Walt broke in. "I'll expect your first report early next week."

"Right." David stood up and stretched. Every muscle in his long frame ached with residual cold. "Is this operation covert, by the way, or do I just knock on Ms. Llewellyn's door and flash my identification?"

Clearly, Walt Zigman had a headache, too. "That was a stupid question, Goddard. You've been on White House Detail too damned long. Spent too much time walking the first lady's dog. Of *course* it's covert!"

David shrugged, feeling weary. Maybe Walt was right; maybe he was getting soft. Instead of thinking about this case on every level, a part of him was anticipating a day at Chris's place. The kids would be watching the Macy's parade on TV. The smell of roasting turkey would be everywhere....

He reached for the dossier. "Can I take this?"

Walt waved impatiently. "Yeah, yeah, that's your copy."

David tucked the file under one arm. He supposed it was the forthcoming holiday that was distracting him, stirring up bittersweet memories and half-formed hopes, making him feel far older than his thirty-four years. He tried to imagine Marleen, his ex-wife, roasting turkey or settling a band of freckle-faced rugrats in front of the tube to watch a Thanksgiving parade and couldn't. "You having dinner here, Walt?" he asked, his hand on the doorknob. "Tomorrow, I mean?"

Zigman grinned around his cigar stub. "Nope. Going to New York to see my daughter. Happy Thanksgiving, Goddard."

David laughed, though he had a bereft feeling inside. He thought of Marleen studying chimpanzees in Borneo and wondered if she remembered that she'd once wanted to raise an entirely different kind of monkey. "I'll call you on Monday."

"Right."

David stepped out into the wide, familiar hallway, with its lighted paintings and expensively shabby carpeting. In front of the Oval Office, two agents guarded the heavy double doors. He nodded and they nodded back, their faces solemn.

Downstairs, David left the White House by a side door, then strode through the snow-dusted parking lot to his car. At one of the high wrought-iron gates, he showed his ID, even though he was going out, not in, even though he knew the young Marines on duty, knew their wives and their kids and their collar sizes.

Again he felt lonely. Even quietly desperate. As the White House gate clanked shut behind him, he turned up the car radio in a belated effort to cover the sound.

Holly Llewellyn placed the elegantly scripted invitation in the center of the kitchen mantelpiece, between the antique Seth Thomas clock and a framed photograph of herself with James Beard. Hands tucked into the pockets of her cozy blue jogging jacket, she stood back to admire it.

"Imagine," said her friend and secretary, Elaine Bateman, from her chair at the cluttered trestle table. "Being invited to the White House! An inaugural ball! Good heavens, Holly, what are you going to wear?"

Holly's bright, aquamarine eyes danced with mischief and she withdrew her hands from her pockets to push her chin-length blond hair atop her head. "Nothing," she crooned, striking a cheesecake pose.

"That ought to cause a sensation!"

Holly made a face and went back to the portable photocopy machine, set up on the end of the trestle table. She began busily feeding in the typewritten pages of "Egg Rolls for a Crowd," the initial chapter of her new book. "I meant that I'm not going," she pointed out. "After all, Toby is in school and I've got my classes to teach and this book to finish. These recipes all have to be tested and retested, you know. And there's my newspaper column—"

"Excuses!" Elaine cried, ignoring the finished manuscript, *Soups are Super*, that she was supposed to be indexing. "Good Lord, Holly, how many times does a person's cousin get elected president? I can't believe you'd miss a chance like this! Besides, you've got until January."

The rhythmic flashing of the photocopier's light was giving Holly a headache; she closed her eyes and ran her hands down the sides of her trim-fitting jeans. "I'm not going," she repeated sharply.

Elaine sighed in a way that made Holly regret her tone of voice. "Okay, Holl. No problem. Listen, tomorrow's Thanksgiving—do you mind if I take this home and work on it there? I've got a turkey to stuff and ceramic pilgrims to set out in strategic places."

Holly laughed, able to look at her friend now. "Go," she said. "And leave the manuscript here. It will keep until Monday."

Elaine beamed triumphantly, gathering the stack of blue-penciled pages into a neat pile. "You were always a soft touch for ceramic pilgrims," she grinned. "Are you sure you don't want me to work Friday?"

"Positive."

Elaine looked worried now, her wide green eyes watchful. "You and Toby have somewhere to go for Thanksgiving, don't you? I mean, you're not going to sit here and brood or anything, are you?"

Holly felt a tender sort of exasperation. "We're spending the day with Skyler's parents, worrywart. Hie thyself home, before that husband of yours tries to stuff the gobbler on his own. Remember last year? He cut himself on the giblets."

Elaine laughed. "Roy means well," she said, taking her coat from the antique wall rack beside the back door. Shrugging into it, she tossed her glossy brown hair back over her shoulders. "How was he to know that a partially frozen turkey neck can be lethal?"

"How indeed?" Holly chuckled, wondering why she felt so sad. Skyler's parents were nice people; she and Toby would both have a good time at their house.

"Happy, happy," Elaine sang, opening the door to leave and letting in a rush of frigid November air. "See you Monday."

"Monday," Holly confirmed, smiling hard. But when her friend was gone, she sat down on the long bench beside the trestle table and sighed.

Just then Toby scrambled in from the other direction, still wearing his jacket, earmuffs and mittens. His "moon" boots made puddles on the red-brick floor, and he was waving a multi-colored construction-paper turkey in one hand. "Look what we made, Mom! Look what we made!"

From somewhere in the depths of her, Holly summoned up another smile. "Wow!" she crowed. She didn't bother to correct the little boy, to remind him that she was his aunt and not his mother. She never did that anymore.

The seven-year-old was trying to peel off his winter garb without crumpling his purple, green, pink and black turkey. The cold glowed in his plump cheeks and his china-blue eyes sparkled.

After ruffling his irresistible corn-silk hair with one hand, Holly aided him by taking the bedraggled, paste-crusted turkey while he wrestled out of his jacket.

"I've never seen a turkey quite like this," she remarked.

Toby laughed and Holly felt a pang at the sound; he was so like her brother, Craig. Poor, hunted Craig. "I wanted him to be diffrent, Mom!" For a moment, the child looked sheepish. "Besides, all the brown and gold and orange paper was gone."

Holly walked to the huge side-by-side refrigerator and attached the turkey to its surface with magnets. To make room, she had to take down the previous month's construction-paper pumpkin. "No matter," she said. "I like this bird. He has character. Are you hungry?"

"Starved," the little boy exclaimed, and there was a scuffling sound as he made a place for himself at the paper-and-book-littered table.

Holly plundered the refrigerator for lunch meat, sliced cheese, lettuce and mustard. She thought ruefully that another trip to the supermarket was in order.

Carrying the armload of sandwich supplies over to the counter, Holly set everything down to open the old-fashioned wooden bread box.

"We're still going to Skyler's place tomorrow, right?" Toby asked without looking at her.

Holly was closing the bread sack, tucking it back into its nook. She sighed. "Not exactly. We're going to his parents' house, remember? They live in the country."

"Oh."

"You don't like Skyler very much, do you Toby?" she ventured, buttering a slice of bread, adding cheese and lunch meat and a lettuce leaf.

"Are you going to marry him?" the child countered, watching Holly with pensive eyes.

It was a fair question, but since Holly didn't know the answer herself, she could hardly offer one to Toby. "I don't know. I like Skyler."

"A lot?"

Holly thought. "Yeah. I like him a lot."

"Do you love him?"

Holly's knife clattered in the mustard jar. "Well—"

"You're supposed to love somebody if you're going to marry them. The way Elaine loves Roy. She's always kissing him and when he says something, she looks at him like every word is real important.''

Holly paused, feeling oddly shaken, and gave her nephew a lopsided grin. ''You've been watching Phil Donahue again,'' she teased.

Toby looked puzzled. ''Huh?''

''Never mind. How was school today?''

The little boy sighed. ''I didn't get any orange paper.''

''I remember,'' Holly replied, putting the finished sandwich on a plate and carrying it to the table. ''How come that happened, anyway? Were you late for art class or something?''

Toby was gathering up the sandwich in eager hands. ''I had to talk to the principal.''

''Toby Llewellyn! Did you get into trouble?''

''No,'' Toby said through a mouthful. ''He wanted me to talk about the new president next week at assembly.''

A jolt of mingled alarm and fury raced through Holly; she had to take a deep breath before she could speak calmly. ''What? How did he know—''

Toby shrugged. ''Maybe there was something in the paper. Mr. Richardson was pretty disappointed when I told him I didn't know the president.''

Holly was pacing the floor, her hands tucked into the hip pockets of her jeans. The celebrity of being a cookbook author was one thing—only a select group of people cared one way or the other, of course—but this shirttail relationship to the future president could get to be a real problem. Suppose reporters started taking an interest? Suppose what Craig had done got talked about? Toby could be hurt or even put in real danger!

"Did you see any newspaper people, Toby? Did anybody ask you questions?"

Toby shook his head. "Can I watch TV?"

Holly nodded somewhat impatiently. "You'll tell me if anyone you don't know tries to talk to you, won't you, Toby?"

"Sure. Is there any lemonade?"

Agitated, Holly forced herself to stop pacing. There was no reason to panic, no reason. After all, she and Craig were only distantly related to the new president.

"Mom?"

"Cocoa. I'll make you a cup of cocoa. It's too cold for lemonade."

"Okay," Toby agreed amiably, on his way out of the kitchen. A moment later, as she searched the cupboard for a saucepan in which to prepare the cocoa, Holly heard the television set in the next room blaring. Her hands trembled as she collected the milk, salt, sugar and chocolate.

*Oh, my God,* she thought. *Craig, what have you done to us? What have you done to all of us?*

She reflected on her brother's problems as she made the cocoa and carried it into the family room to Toby. The telephone shrilled and Holly jumped, startled out of her skin. She raced back into the kitchen and grabbed up the receiver. "H-hello?"

"Hello, kitten," said the familiar masculine voice on the other end.

Holly sank into the chair at her small desk, her knees wobbly. Skyler. It was only Skyler. She was so glad that she didn't even ask him not to call her by that silly, condescending nickname. "Hi," she said.

Skyler cleared his throat. Skyler always cleared his throat when he was about to suggest something he expected Holly to oppose. "Listen, Holl, I was wondering—why don't you and I and the kid just drive up to my folks' place tonight, instead of waiting until tomorrow? I could close the shop early."

Holly bit her lower lip, considering. She hated the way Skyler always referred to Toby as "the kid," as though he didn't have a name. But confronting him about it had about as much effect as asking him not to call her "kitten." Which was none at all.

"Holly?" Skyler prompted when the silence grew too long. "Are you still there?"

"I was just—I was just thinking."

"Is it that hard to decide?" he snapped, impatient now.

Holly drew a deep breath and let it out slowly before answering. "No, Skyler, of course not. But, well—"

Skyler made an exasperated sound. "I suppose you're afraid I'll expect you to sleep with me. In my parents' house, Holly? Give me some credit, will you?"

He was being unusually defensive, Holly thought, but then sex was an issue between them. While Holly was certainly no innocent, she wasn't ready for that kind of intimacy, not with Skyler Hollis at any rate. "Sky."

"Well? That is what you were thinking, isn't it?"

Holly sighed as she rubbed her aching temples with a thumb and forefinger. "Yes. And I refuse to discuss it over the telephone."

Skyler's struggle for equanimity was almost audible. "Right," he said presently. "Do I pick you up tonight or not, Holly?"

"What time would we leave?"

"I can be ready in about an hour and a half. We could eat dinner on the way if you'd like."

Holly found herself smiling in spite of the odd tension Skyler always managed to inspire in her. "That sounds like a good idea. I really don't feel like cooking."

Skyler chuckled. "Little wonder."

"On the other hand, I've got a freezer full of experimental egg rolls. Test run from yesterday."

"I'm in no mood to be a guinea pig," Skyler retorted quickly, and there was a disturbing note of conviction in his voice. "I'll see you at," he paused and Holly could imagine him looking at his thin gold watch, "six-thirty."

"Six-thirty," Holly confirmed, and after a few perfunctory words of parting, they both hung up.

Somebody should have said, "I love you," Holly thought as she left the kitchen.

Skyler stood before the mantelpiece, frowning at the invitation to the Inaugural Ball. He was a tall man with sleek, fair hair, an altar-boy face and elegant, long-fingered hands. The owner of a very successful stereo-and-television dealership, Skyler was prosperous, and his tailored gray slacks and tasteful cashmere sweater were meant to convey that to even the most casual onlooker.

Holly stood watching him, waiting, her hands in the pockets of her black corduroy culotte. With it she wore high leather boots, a burgundy blouse and her black velvet blazer. Her hair, cut in a layered, easy-care style, glistened, and her makeup was perfect.

"You didn't tell me you knew—" Skyler began, pensively, turning to frown at her.

"I know lots of famous people, Skyler."

"Yes," Skyler mused, one perfect golden eyebrow arched in speculation, "but shaking somebody's hand on *The Merv Griffin Show* and getting invited to an Inaugural Ball are two different things."

Holly folded her arms and allowed herself a wry smile, though inside she felt shaky. She always did with Skyler; his very presence seemed to evaporate her self-confidence. "Howard is a distant cousin, Skyler. I didn't mention it because I didn't think it mattered."

"Howard! You call the next president of the United States 'Howard'?"

Holly shrugged. "It's his name, Skyler."

"Still—"

Suddenly Holly was impatient. "I'm not going to the ball anyway," she said, reaching for her purse, which sat on the corner of her desk. "Shall we go? The traffic will be horrendous and it's still snowing."

Skyler nodded distractedly, but even as they left the kitchen, he kept casting his eyes back to the invitation. "Right," he said.

Once Toby and his suitcase, which also contained Holly's things, had been tucked into the tiny backseat of Skyler's sleek, sporty car, and the boy had been carefully buckled in by a seat belt, Holly glanced quickly at her old-fashioned brick house and felt a sweeping, dismal sort of loneliness.

Mentally, she shook herself. Good heavens, she was acting as though she would never see her cozy home again.

The traffic, as Holly had predicted, was terrible. The number of cars leaving the city was equaled only by the number of cars coming in, and the snow swirled and spiraled in front of the windshield, making it almost impossible to see.

"We're in hyperspace!" Toby cried in delight. Out of the corner of her eye, Holly saw Skyler grimace and tighten his grasp on the steering wheel.

She let her head rest against the back of the seat and closed her eyes. Skyler Hollis was what her mother might have called a "catch," with his good looks and his flourishing business, but his antipathy toward Toby, carefully hidden though it was, disturbed Holly. She wondered if he felt that way about all children or just her nephew in particular.

An hour and a half later, when they had eaten at a roadside restaurant and were again on their way, Toby asleep in the back seat, she broached the subject. "Do you want children, Skyler?"

He glanced at her and then turned his attention back to the hazardous road. "Of my own? Most men do, Holly."

Holly sat up a little straighter. "Of my own," he'd said. "In other words, you wouldn't accept Toby?"

Skyler's clean-shaven jaw worked for a moment, and his narrow shoulders grew tense. "Your brother will probably come back for him one day, Holly. You told me that yourself."

Holly sighed and looked out the window at the fierce flurries of snow. She had told Skyler that, it was true. But now she had grave doubts that her brother would ever actually reclaim his son or be in a position to take care of him. After all, Toby's mother was dead, and though few people knew it, Craig was a wanted man, suspected of espionage. It was possible, in fact, that he wasn't even in the country.

"Craig won't come back," she said quietly, after a long silence.

"How could he not come back?" Skyler demanded angrily. "You've got his kid!"

His kid. When Skyler said that, used those simple, everyday words, it always sounded inhumane. "And I want to keep him, Skyler. Craig is in no position to be a real father and besides, I love Toby. I love him very, very much."

There seemed to be nothing to say after that. Skyler shoved a classical tape into the slot on the dashboard and the car was filled with thunderous Beethoven.

Chris's kitchen was a bright, warm, cluttered place. The walls were graced with shining copper utensils and a fire crackled in the huge wood-burning stove in one corner of the room. Two long shelves held the largest collection of cookbooks David had ever seen.

Frowning, he took down a copy of *Fun With Tacos* and studied the colored photograph of the author on the back cover. Tousled, honey-colored hair, enormous blue-green eyes. Holly Llewellyn.

"Taking up the culinary arts?" Chris asked mischievously, standing beside him.

Startled, David thrust the thin volume back into its place on the shelf and shook his head.

Chris, a lovely woman with dark hair and eyes, laughed warmly and hugged her brother. "We live in a new age, you know. Men are actually cooking, among other things."

A new age. David's mind caught on those words— he was uneasy, even jumpy. He had the strangest feeling that he was on the edge of something momentous, something that would change his life forever. He took Holly Llewellyn's cookbook down from the shelf again, turned it over and studied the captivating face on the back.

Llewellyn, he thought, if you turn out to be a fink, I'm not going to be able to take it.

## Chapter Two

Holly looked with a jaundiced eye at the mechanical department-store Santa Claus nodding beside the escalator. Thanksgiving is over, she thought ruefully, so bring on Christmas.

In the toy section to her left, a horde of shoppers were engaged in a good-natured battle of some sort.

Reaching the next floor and the cookware section of the large store, Holly found Elaine already there, her hair pinned to the top of her head, a clipboard in hand.

"What's going on downstairs?" Holly asked irritably. The weekend with Skyler and his parents had been a disaster.

Elaine chuckled but did not look up from the list she was going over. "They got in a shipment of Cabbage Patch dolls."

Shrugging out of her winter coat, Holly assessed the room. The store had done a good job of setting up; there were tables, aprons and even chefs' hats for all the students. In the cooking area, where Holly would demonstrate the fine art of baking fruitcake, an assortment of copper utensils had been set out on the counter.

She peered at Elaine's clipboard. Normally, twelve students were accepted for her popular cooking classes, but this time the list showed thirteen names. "David Goddard? Who the devil is that?"

Elaine gave her friend and employer an understanding, patient look. "There's always room for one more, right?" she grinned. "The guy was so eager...."

Holly was annoyed and tired. All she wanted to do was spend the night at home, in front of the TV or better yet, in a hot bath with a book. Anywhere but in this posh downtown department store, teaching thirteen people how to bake fruitcake. "Elaine," she began stiffly, "this is a popular class. There is a waiting list several months long, in case you've forgotten. So where do you get off letting some bozo walk in and sign up just because he's eager?"

Elaine colored prettily. "Actually, he's better than eager. He's a hunk."

"Great! You let him in because he was good-looking!"

Elaine shrugged. "What can I tell you? I looked up into those navy-blue eyes and I could not deny the man ten lessons and chef's hat."

Holly muttered an expletive and flung down her purse and coat. "I'll be glad to deny him for you," she snapped, washing her hands at the gleaming steel sink that was part of the store's fully equipped kitchen. "Where is he?"

"Downstairs, I think, in the toy department," Elaine replied, unruffled, as she checked the supplies of flour, sugar and assorted other ingredients against another list on her clipboard. "He said something about buying a couple of those dolls for his nieces."

Holly found an apron and put it on over her jeans and plaid cotton blouse. Despite repeated pleas from the store's publicity director, she refused to wear a chef's hat. "I don't know why I agree to do these cooking classes, anyway," she muttered.

"You have a contract with the store," came the blithe reply from her secretary. "And they pay you big bucks."

"Thanks for reminding me."

Elaine looked up from her clipboard and made a face. "Anytime, boss."

Holly couldn't help it; she had to grin. "I don't know how you put up with me. I've been a grouch all day and I'm sorry."

Elaine sighed. "A weekend with Skyler Hollis would do that to anybody. Everything checks out, Holly. Could I go now? Roy and I are going to have dinner out and then do some early shopping."

"Go. Leave me here to tell the hunk that he can't learn to bake fruitcake." Holly paused and assumed a pose of mock despondency. "The help you get these days."

Elaine laughed. "When you see him, you'll let him stay. Believe me, God was in a good mood the day He threw this dude together. Everything is definitely in the right place."

"Elaine Bateman, you are a happily married woman!"

The pretty brunette was pulling on her coat. "Yeah. But I'm not blind," she twinkled, before taking up her purse and starting off toward the escalators.

Holly was alone for about five minutes, and then a heavy, earnest-looking man arrived. She asked his name—it was Alvin Parkins—and checked it off on Elaine's list. One by one, the other students came, some of them bringing copies of Holly's books to be autographed.

And then he showed up. Number Thirteen. The intruder. At the very first sight of him, Holly's stomach did a nervous flip.

He was tall and his hair was very dark, neatly cut, and his eyes were a piercing navy blue, just as Elaine had said. He wore blue jeans, a soft white sweater and a brown leather jacket and under each of his powerful arms, he carried a box containing a Cabbage Patch doll.

Holly lifted her chin, squared her shoulders and approached him. "Mr. Goddard?"

He tilted his head slightly, in acknowledgment or greeting or both. His cologne was musky and Holly found herself trying to identify it by name.

Holly glanced at the dolls in their yellow boxes, trying to delay the moment when she must tell this man that there simply wasn't room for him in the fruitcake class. "Mr. Goddard—I—" her eyes widened. "Why, those dolls are black!"

David Goddard arched one dark eyebrow. "Are you prejudiced, Ms. Llewellyn?" he asked lightly.

"Of course not!" Holly bridled, reddening. "It's just that...well...white children usually want white dolls, just as black children want black ones."

Shoulders fit for a linebacker moved in a leather-shrouded shrug. "I'll tell my nieces that they're distant cousins to Michael Jackson," he offered blithely.

Holly cleared her throat. How had she gotten on this subject, anyway? What did she care if David Goddard bought black dolls or white? "The fact is, Mr. Goddard, that there just isn't...there just isn't room in this class for another person. I'm sorry."

He set the dolls down on one of the tables and calmly removed his jacket. He didn't look as though he planned to go anywhere. "I'm sorry, too. That it's a problem, I mean. But your secretary took my money and told me I had a place in good old Fruitcake 101 and I'm staying."

Holly felt the color rising in her face. "You're going to be difficult, aren't you?"

David Goddard smiled and folded his arms, stirring that appealing musky scent and touching something deep inside Holly. "If necessary," came the simple reply.

To hide her annoyance, Holly looked down at her watch. It was time to start the class and all the other students were there, ready to begin. It wouldn't do to make a scene in front of them and besides, Elaine had told the man he could participate. "All right, then," she muttered, "you can stay."

"Thank you," he replied, and the deep warmth in his voice soothed Holly somehow, taking away the anger that had arisen at his stubbornness.

David Goddard proved to be an attentive student, listening closely to every word Holly said, watching every move she made. She could almost feel the steel-trap agility of his mind.

When the class was over and Holly was cleaning up, he stayed behind to help. Without a word he rolled up his sleeves and began running hot water into the sink.

Holly gathered mixing bowls and spatulas and breadpans and brought them to the counter. It was odd, the feeling she had—as though they were old friends instead of strangers, washing dishes together in a homey kitchen instead of a busy department store.

"This is quite a setup," he remarked, up to his elbows in hot, soapy water.

Holly found herself smiling. "I know. I was impressed the first time I saw it, too." *And the first time I saw you, Number Thirteen.*

"Did they put all this in just for you?"

She shook her head and took a dish towel from a top drawer. "I think it was a demonstration kitchen at first—you know, so people could see how the appliances would look in a home setting. When I started to become well-known, Cookware and Books put their heads together and came up with the idea that I should teach classes here."

David smiled. He had a nice smile, she noted, a smile touched with humor. Full of straight white teeth. But what was that sad detachment in the depths of his ink-blue eyes?

"Doesn't that take up a lot of your time? Teaching, I mean?" he asked.

Holly dried a lacquered copper mixing bowl to a red-gold shine. She liked the way it looked, so bright and cheery. "I guess it does. I travel a little, write my books. And I keep up a weekly newspaper column, too." She paused, then shrugged. "I like teaching, though. I get to meet new people that way."

"You don't meet people when you travel?"

She smiled again, wearily. "Not really. I take classes in other countries, and sometimes I'm the only student. It's precise, exhausting work and I usually don't even get to see the sights, let alone strike up lasting friendships. What do you do for a living, Mr. Goddard?"

"Call me David or I'll never tell," he retorted, and even though his glance was pleasant, Holly had a feeling that he was stalling, for some reason.

"All right. What do you do for a living, David?" she insisted, watching him.

The navy-blue eyes were suddenly averted; he was concentrating on scrubbing a baking pan. "I'm in law school at Gonzaga," he finally answered.

The answer seemed incomplete somehow. David Goddard was in his mid-thirties, unless Holly missed her guess. Surely old enough to be through with college, even law school. On the other hand, lots of people changed careers these days. "What kind of lawyer are you planning to be? Corporate? Criminal?"

He took up another baking pan. "Actually, I'm taking review courses. I graduated several years ago, but I haven't been practising. I thought I'd better brush up a little before I tackled the Bar Exam again."

"The Bar Exam? I thought you only had to take that once."

"It varies from state to state. I didn't study in Washington."

He was hedging; Holly was sure of it. But why? "Where did you study?"

David still would not look at her. "Virginia. Do they pay you extra for washing dishes?"

The sudden shift in the conversation unsettled Holly, as did something she sensed in this man. In a flash it occurred to her that he might be a very clever reporter looking for a story. Her cooking career usually didn't generate a lot of interest, but being third cousin to the next president of the United States just might. And what if he knew about Craig?

Holly paled and withrew a little. "I can finish this myself," she said stiffly. "Why don't you go?"

Now the inky gaze was fixed on her, impaling her, touching that hidden something that did not want to be touched. "Is there a sudden chill in here or am I imagining it?" he countered.

Holly kept her distance. Gone was the feeling of companionship she had enjoyed earlier. There was danger in this man; there was watchfulness. Why hadn't she noticed that before? She fielded his question with one of her own. "Why would a lawyer want to learn to bake fruitcake?" she asked.

David went right on washing, his hands swift and strong at the task. "For the same reasons the other people in this class do, Holly. There was a bookkeeper, if I remember correctly, and a construction worker—"

"Maybe a journalist or two," she put in sharply, glaring at him now.

"A journalist?" He looked honestly puzzled for a moment, and then a light dawned in the blue depths of his eyes. "You think I'm a reporter," he said.

"Are you?"

"No," came the firm and immediate reply. And Holly believed David Goddard, though she couldn't have explained why.

"You really want to bake fruitcake?" Did she sound eager? Lord, she hoped not.

David laughed and touched the tip of her nose with a sudsy index finger. "I really want to bake fruitcake."

They finished cleaning up and David lingered while Holly put on her coat and reached for her purse.

"Was there something else?" she asked, trying to keep her voice level. For some reason Number Thirteen had a strange effect on her.

"Yes," he answered. "I plan to walk you to your car. It's late and I don't want you to get mugged."

Holly felt warm. Protected. Though she cherished her independence, it was nice to have someone looking out for her that way. "Thank you," she said.

Her car was in a parking tower in the next block, isolated and in shadow. It probably wasn't safe, walking there alone, but she hadn't thought of that in her hurry to get to the store and conduct her class. She was glad David was with her.

He waited beside her sporty blue Toyota until she had found her keys, unlocked the door and slid behind the wheel. Toby's model airplane, a miniature Cessna flown by remote control, was on the seat, and she moved it in order to set down her purse and the small notebook she always carried.

"Is that yours?" David asked with interest, his eyes on the expensive toy.

"Actually," grinned Holly, "it belongs to my nephew, though I do admit to flying it now and then up at Manito Park."

Again there was an unsettling alertness in David, as though he was cataloguing the information for future reference. But why would he do such a thing?

"I have a plane like that," he said, and Holly ascribed her instant impression that he was lying to weariness and an overactive imagination.

David Goddard was a kind, attractive man, not a reporter or an FBI agent. She was going to have to stop letting her fancy take over at every turn or she would become paranoid. She said good-bye, started the car and backed out of her parking space.

There was a light snow falling and Holly drove up the steep South Hill at a cautious pace, her mind staying behind with David Goddard.

He *could* be a reporter, she thought distractedly as she navigated the slick, slushy streets. He could even be an FBI agent hoping to find Craig.

Holly laughed at herself and shook her head. "You'd better take up writing fiction, Llewellyn," she said aloud. "You've got the imagination for it."

But even as she pulled the car to a stop in her own driveway, even as she turned off the engine and gathered up her purse, her notebook and Toby's airplane from the seat, she couldn't shake the conviction that David Goddard was something more than a second-time law student who liked to cook.

Inside the house, Holly found her housekeeper and favorite baby-sitter working happily in front of the living-room fireplace. Madge Elkins was a middle-aged woman, still trim and attractive, and her consuming passion was entering contests.

Now, she was busily writing her name and address on one plain white 3-by-5-inch piece of paper after another.

"What are you going to win this time, Madge?" Holly asked pleasantly, putting down the things she carried and getting out of her snow-dampened coat.

"A computer system," Madge replied, tucking a paper into an envelope and sealing it with a flourish. "Printer, software, monitor, the whole shebang."

Another person might have laughed, but Holly had known Madge for several years and in that time had seen her win more than one impressive prize in contests. A car, for instance, and a mink coat. "Is Toby sleeping?"

"Like the proverbial log," Madge answered, gathering a stack of envelopes, all addressed and stamped, into a stack. "You had a couple of phone calls—one from Skyler and one from a man who wouldn't leave his name."

Again Holly felt uneasy. "What did he say? The man who wouldn't give you his name, I mean?"

Madge shrugged, fussing with her contest paraphernalia. "Just that he'd call back. Skyler wants you to call him."

Holly was suddenly testy. If Skyler wanted to talk to her, he could darned well call back. She saw Madge to the door and then headed off toward the kitchen, planning to take one of her experiments out of the freezer and zap it in the microwave. She'd been running late before cooking class and hadn't had a chance to eat dinner.

Just as the bell on the microwave chimed, so did the telephone. Muttering, Holly dived for the receiver, afraid that the ringing of the upstairs extension would awaken Toby.

"Hello?" she demanded impatiently.

The voice on the other end of the line was haunted, shaky. "Sis?"

Holly's knees gave out and she sank into the chair at the desk. "Craig! Where are you? What—"

Her brother laughed nervously and the sound was broken and humorless, painful to hear. "Never mind where I am. You know I can't tell you that. Your phone might be bugged or something."

"Craig, don't be paranoid. Where are you?"

"Let's just say that this call isn't long-distance from the Kremlin. How's Toby?"

Holly deliberately calmed herself, measuring her tones. She was desperate not to panic Craig and cause him to hang up. "Toby is fine, Craig. How about you?"

"I'm all right. A little tired. More than a little broke."

Holly closed her eyes. So that was the reason for his call. Money. Why was she always surprised by that? "And you need a few bucks."

"You can spare it, can't you?" Craig sounded petulant, far younger than his thirty-six years. "You're a rich lady, sis. Didn't I see you on *Donahue* a few months ago?"

"Craig, come home. Please?"

He made a bitter, contemptuous sound. "And do what? Turn myself in, Holly? Give me a break—I'll be in prison for the rest of my life!"

"Maybe not. Craig, you're not well. You need help. And I promise that I'll stand by you."

"If you want to stand by me, little sister, just send a cashier's check to the usual place. And do it tomorrow if you don't want me to lose weight."

"Craig, listen to me—"

"Just send the money," he barked, and then the line went dead. Holly sat for five minutes, letting her egg roll get cold in the microwave, holding the telephone receiver in her hand and just staring into space.

Finally she hung up, forced herself out of the chair, and took the egg roll from the microwave. Although she ate, she tasted nothing at all. The egg rolls she had taken such pride in making might as well have been filled with sawdust.

David Goddard locked the two Cabbage Patch dolls into the trunk of his rented car, shaking his head as he remembered the way he'd had to scramble for them. He sighed, then grinned. The kids would like them, so it had been worth a few scars.

On his way back to the parking garage's lonely elevator, he passed the place where Holly's Toyota had been. Instantly, his mind and all his senses brimmed with the scent and image of her.

He reached the elevator and punched the button with an annoyed motion of his right hand. Walt Zigman was full of sheep-dip if he thought that woman was capable of espionage. Holly Llewellyn was harried and she was haunted, but she was nobody's flunky.

The elevator ground to a stop; the doors swished open. David stepped inside and punched another button. He smiled to himself, thinking of the first fruitcake he'd ever put together in his life. It was a good thing no one had bothered to taste it; his cover would have been blown then and there. He'd been too lost in Holly Llewellyn's aquamarine eyes to concentrate on baking.

Baking. He rolled his eyes. For this I went to law school, he thought. For this I walked the first lady's dog.

He reached the first floor of the parking garage, where there was a wine shop and an old-fashioned ice cream parlor. Ice cream, in this weather? David shivered and lifted his collar before stepping back outside, onto the street.

At the corner, he paused. Gung ho Christmas shoppers surged past him when the light changed, carrying him along. He went back into the department store where Holly had taught her class and again braved the toy department. This time he bought an airplane, a model that would fly by means of a small hand-control unit. Manito Park, she'd said.

Half an hour later David entered his apartment, acquired only two days before, with mingled relief and reluctance. It was a small place, furnished in tacky plaids. The carpet was thin and the last tenant had owned a dog, judging by the oval stains by the door and in front of the fold-out sofa bed. At least he had a telephone. David went to it and, with perverse pleasure, punched out Walt Zigman's home number.

It was after one in the morning on the east coast and Walt's voice was a groggy rumble. "Who the—"

"Goddard," David said crisply, grinning. "I said I'd report Monday. This is my report."

Zigman swore fiercely. "Goddard, did anybody ever tell you that you're a son of a—"

"I met her."

"Holly Llewellyn?" Walt's interest was immediate. Clearly, he was now wide awake. "How did you manage that so fast?"

"Simple. I bought yesterday's paper and read the food section. There was a write-up about her new class."

"Her new class in what?"

David closed his eyes. There was no way out of this one. "Fruitcake," he answered reluctantly.

Zigman laughed. "Fitting," came his rapid-fire reply, just as David had expected.

"You're getting corny in your old age, Walt."

"Did you find out anything?"

David unzipped his jacket and flung it down on the couch. It covered the dolls and the model airplane in its colorful box—he'd be up half the night assembling that sucker. "Sure," he snapped. "She fed me grapes and poured out the whole sordid story of her life in the underworld."

"Don't be a smart—"

"I met her. That's all. But I can tell you this much, Walt: she's no traitor. I'm wasting my time here."

"You're getting paid for it. Keep your eye on the ball, Goddard. When it's time for you to come back to D.C. and follow the new first lady around, I'll let you know."

This time it was David who swore. "Tell me, Walt," he began dryly, "does she have a dog?"

"Three of them," said Walt with obnoxious satisfaction. "By the time the new first family takes up residence, you'll be back on good old Pennsylvania Avenue, passing out poochie treats."

"You're funny as hell, you know that? In fact, why don't you take your goddamned job and—"

"Goddard, Goddard," Walt reprimanded in his favorite fatherly tone. "Calm down, I was just kidding you, that's all. You're a damned good agent."

Agent. If he hadn't felt like screaming swearwords, David would have laughed. "I didn't work my way through law school so that I could walk dogs, Walt."

"You really are unhappy, aren't you?"

"In a word, yes."

"We've been through this before."

"Yeah. Good night, Walt."

"Goddard!"

David hung up.

After a few minutes he hoisted himself up off the fold-out couch, dug the dolls out from under his coat and set them on the scarred counter that separated his living room-bedroom from the cubicle the landlady called a kitchen.

Thinking of his nieces and how they were going to enjoy those dolls, he began to feel better. He bent forward and studied the face of one of them and then the other. The one on the right did look a little bit like Michael Jackson.

"So sing or something," he said, just to fill the silence.

Presently, David took a TV dinner out of the tiny freezer above his refrigerator and shoved it into the doll-sized oven. While it was cooking, he stripped off his clothes, went into the bathroom and wedged himself into a shower designed for a midget. After drying off with one of the three scratchy towels the landlady had seen fit to lend him, he went back to the living room and dug his robe out of a suitcase. Someday, he promised himself, he was going to write a book about the glamorous life of a Secret Service Agent.

After consuming the TV dinner, he set about putting the model airplane together. It was after midnight when he finally gave up, washed the glue from his fingers, folded out the sofa bed and collapsed, falling into an instant sleep.

## Chapter Three

It was very bad luck that, after a quick visit to her bank that bleak Tuesday morning, Holly encountered David in the neighborhood branch of the post office. Or was it luck?

Holly looked at the huge, carefully wrapped parcel in his arms and decided he was only mailing the dolls he'd bought the night before to his nieces. No doubt he lived nearby and it made sense that he would be here.

"Don't you have classes today?" she asked as they waited in line, stiff pleasantries already exchanged.

David smiled wanly. "One o'clock," he answered. He hadn't looked at the address on the envelope Holly carried, as far as she could tell, but she held it against her coat all the same.

Soon enough, it was Holly's turn at the window; she laid the envelope addressed to Craig's go-between girlfriend on the counter and asked that it be registered. While she filled out the form and paid the small fee, David had ample opportunity to study the address, but there was no helping that. She couldn't very well turn around and say, "Please don't look at this envelope. I'm sending money to my brother, who is a fugitive, you see, and there is a chance that you might be a reporter or even an FBI agent." So she said nothing.

"See you tonight?" David asked in a deep quiet voice as she turned away from the window to leave.

Holly hadn't even thought about the classes; she'd been too intent on getting that cashier's check sent off to Craig. "Tonight," she confirmed, but her mind was on the letter she had just mailed. It would reach its destination, Los Angeles, within a day or so. Had she done the wrong thing by making it easier for Craig to keep on running? She knew she had.

She would have left then, but David caught her arm in one hand and stayed her. "Are you all right?" he asked, ignoring the impatient post office clerk, who was waiting to weigh and stamp the package he still held.

Holly nodded quickly and then fled. In her car, she let her forehead rest against the steering wheel for a moment before starting the engine and driving away. As she pulled into a supermarket parking lot a few minutes later, she was still trembling. She loved Craig; he was her brother. But she almost wished the FBI would catch him. That way there wouldn't be any more lying, any more hiding, any more guilt.

She got out of the car, locking it behind her, and went into the supermarket. Think about the sweet-and-sour chicken you've got to test today, she told herself. Think about the spices you'll need. Don't think about Craig and especially don't think about David Goddard. It was a coincidence that he was in the post office just when you were. It was a coincidence!

That seemed unlikely, but by the time she had chosen a cart and gotten out her shopping list, Holly had convinced herself that she was being fanciful again. Paranoid, like Craig.

He was wearing a navy-blue football jersey with white numbers, jeans and polished leather boots. Holly, exhausted from a day of making sweet-and-sour chicken over and over again, gave herself a mental shake. What did she care what David Goddard wore, for heaven's sake?

Her beautiful aquamarine eyes looked hollow and smudges of fatigue and worry darkened the flawless skin beneath. David ached for her. Things were going to get worse, maybe a lot worse, for Holly Llewellyn before they got better.

If they ever got better.

Again he lingered, quietly helping her with the mess left behind by thirteen people struggling with a complicated German recipe. I'll have to go through this eight more times, Holly thought dismally. All the rest of this week. All of next week.

"Coffee?" David asked, drying his hands on one of the pristine towels provided by the store.

Holly found the idea oddly appealing, considering that, on at least one level, she was afraid of David Goddard. "I don't know, I…"

"Please?"

She felt the pull of his blatant masculinity and tried to field it with words. "You didn't take your fruit-cake home last night," she said. "The janitor must have thrown it away."

David folded his arms and arched one eyebrow. He saw through what she was doing; she just knew it. "I threw it away myself," he replied, watching her. "I was afraid you might taste it and flunk me on the spot. Now, are we going for coffee or not?"

Holly couldn't help the nervous, weary chuckle that escaped her. "I'll make you a cup at my place." Now what made her say that? She never brought men to her house; only Skyler came there and he usually invited himself.

"Great," agreed the alarming David Goddard before she could take back the offer. "I'll follow you in my car."

Holly put on her coat, thinking that the kitchen table at home was still littered with reference books and parts of the manuscript Elaine had been indexing all day. The remains of that day's sweet-and-sour chicken experiments probably covered the counters, since Madge wasn't supposed to clean until the next morning; tonight she was only baby-sitting.

Reaching the parking garage, Holly was jarred to find that David's car was next to her own. Not for the first time, she had the unsettling feeling that he always knew where she was and what she was doing. But that was silly. He was a gentleman, that was all. A rare enough animal these days.

"You wanted to make sure I didn't get mugged," she guessed distractedly as he unlocked the door of a small, ordinary brown sedan.

David executed a teasing salute, but Holly was looking at his other hand. The car keys he held were affixed to a chain bearing the insignia of a nationally known rental agency. He rented his car? That seemed odd, just as the vehicle itself was odd, unsuited to him in a myriad of vague ways.

Puzzled, Holly got into her own car, started the ignition and, doubts notwithstanding, led the way to her sizable "cottage" on Spokane's quietly elegant South Hill.

"You rent your car," she said the moment they were in her living room. Not "welcome to my house," not "take off your coat," but "you rent your car." Holly felt stupid.

"Yes," David confessed readily. "Mine is in the shop."

Of course, Holly thought, but she was still bothered on a subliminal, barely discernible level. She drew a deep breath and forced herself to smile. "About that coffee I offered. This way to the kitchen."

David followed her across the shadowy living room, lit only by the dying fire in the hearth, and even though he was walking behind her, she was aware that he was taking in a tremendous amount of information just by looking around.

"Be prepared for a mess," she chimed, to cover her uneasiness. "My assistant and I spent the day making sweet-and-sour chicken."

They entered the kitchen and Holly stopped so swiftly that David nearly collided with her from behind; she felt the hard wall of his body touch her and glance quickly away.

Madge was at the sink, just finishing an impromptu cleaning detail, but her presence wasn't what caught Holly so off-guard. Skyler was sitting at the table, sipping coffee. Why hadn't she noticed his car outside?

He looked up and there was a challenge in his brown eyes as they assessed David Goddard. "I don't believe we've met," he said coldly, rising from the bench at Holly's table to glare at David.

Skyler was acting like a jealous husband and it infuriated Holly, but before she could say anything at all David crossed the room and extended his hand to Skyler.

"David Goddard," he said in crisp introduction.

Madge took in the scene with bright, interested eyes, but did not say anything. Neither did Holly, who was too taken aback by the intangible storm that was suddenly raging in her quiet, cozy kitchen.

"Skyler Hollis," came the grudging reponse.

David took in Skyler's sleek blond hair, elegant green sweater and custom-made slacks in one swift, indigo sweep. "Did you ever appear on the *Lawrence Welk Show*?" he asked.

Madge made a chortling sound and turned back to the sink. Holly rolled her eyes heavenward and then stomped over to the counter, where the coffee maker waited.

"I own a stereo store," Skyler announced, either missing the reference to his wholesome good looks or choosing to ignore it. "What do you do, Goddard?"

David, Holly saw in a quick glance over one shoulder, gave a slow smile. "I'm learning to make fruitcake."

"Fruitcake," Skyler huffed, scowling. "I meant, what do you do for a living?"

"I'm a door-to-door salesman," was the icy and totally false reply. "I sell air fresheners. You know, those little bowls with the flowers in them—"

"Here's your coffee," Holly broke in archly, setting David's cup down on the just-cleared trestle table with a resounding thump. "Skyler, do you need a refill?"

Skyler shot her a look and carried his cup to the sink, where he thrust it into the hands of a sedately amused Madge Elkins. "No!" he barked.

"Am I breaking up a meaningful relationship?" David asked, lifting his cup in an unsuccessfull attempt to hide a grin.

Skyler's look darkened; he leaned back against the counter and stubbornly folded his arms.

Holly was embarrassed and exasperated. "Skyler Hollis, will you just sit down, please? David is—"

"I know what Davis is," Skyler snapped before he stomped out of the kitchen. Seconds later, the front door slammed.

"I'm sorry," David said.

"I could swear I saw smoke coming out of that man's ears," Madge put in, receiving a swift look from Holly for her trouble.

The housekeeper smiled and shrugged, then took her leave without waiting for an introduction to David Goddard.

They were alone. Holly sighed heavily and fixed her gaze on her own cup of coffee.

"Are you in love with Skyler—what's his name? Hollis?"

The directness of the question brought Holly's gaze shooting up from the dark brew in her cup to David's face. "In love with him?" she echoed stupidly.

"You do realize, I hope, that if you marry that guy your name will be Holly Hollis?"

Holly burst out laughing. "You know, I never thought of that. I guess I'd just have to go on calling myself Llewellyn."

David's impossibly blue eyes were filled with gentle humor. "I really am sorry if I caused any trouble, Holly. If you want me to apologize to Hollis, I will."

"No," Holly said quickly. Perhaps too quickly. "Skyler had no right to act that way," she added moments later, in more carefully measured tones. "He has no claim on me and if I want to bring a friend home for coffee..."

"Is that what I am, Holly? Your friend?"

Holly clasped her hands together in her lap. She was twenty-seven years old, an adult, but she suddenly felt like a fifteen-year-old on her first date. "I hope so," she said softly.

Graciously, David changed the subject. The muscles in his forearms worked as he reached for the sugar bowl and added a spoonful to his coffee. "You aren't even thirty yet, unless I miss my guess," he said. "How did you happen to accomplish so much by such a tender age?"

Holly was comfortable with the subject of her career, at least. She pushed aside the strange suspicions she had about this man who sat across the table from her and allowed herself to forget, for a little while, her worries about Craig and her impossible relationship with Skyler Hollis. "I was lucky. My grandmother wrote cookbooks, you know, and she taught me a lot. And I worked hard."

"You must have spent a lot of time with your grandmother," David remarked, watching her.

"My brother and I lived with her, along with our mother. Our father was killed in an accident when I was seven," Holly blurted out in a rush. There, she thought. If he asks about Craig, I'll know something is wrong.

She held her breath.

"Your mother and grandmother are both gone now?" David asked gently.

Holly was unaccountably relieved, though her throat tightened when she answered. "Grandmother passed away, yes. Mother married a missionary doctor and we don't see her very often."

David's rugged face seemed to grow taut for a moment. "You've never been married?"

Holly shook her head. "I almost was, once." Strange. She could think of Ben now, without hurting. "What about you?"

David laughed, but there was no amusement in the sound or in the ink-blue flash of his eyes. Holly knew before he spoke that he'd once been hurt, and very badly. "I got married during my second year of law school," he said. "Marleen was a graduate student in Animal Sciences."

There was anger as well as pain in his voice. Holly deduced that Marleen had not died, as Ben had. "And?" she prompted.

"And she's now in Borneo studying chimps. She finds them endlessly fascinating and far less demanding, I would imagine, than a husband."

The bitterness in his tone stung Holly profoundly. David still loved Marleen despite his anger; she was sure of it. And for some reason, that hurt. "I'm sorry," she said, getting up hastily to go to the coffee maker and bring the decanter back to the table, where she refilled her own cup and then David's.

"Don't be," David replied succinctly. "Marleen is happy."

"But what about you?" Holly wanted to ask, though, of course, she didn't dare. She put sugar into her coffee—something she never did—and kept her eyes averted.

"You said you were almost married once. What happened, Holly?"

Holly's throat constricted again. "My fiancé was killed," she managed to say. "He was working on a construction project in Alaska and...and he fell."

"You loved him a lot, didn't you?"

Holly nodded. "I wanted to die, too, at the time. And I was so angry."

There was a short, companionable silence. The coffee maker made gurgling sounds and the fire crackled on the kitchen hearth. David's hand came, strong and warm, across the tabletop, to shelter Holly's hand.

It was then that Toby shuffled into the kitchen, looking sleepy and rumpled in his cherished Spiderman pajamas. "Is it time to go to school, Mom?" he asked, befuddled.

Holly's eyes darted involutarily to David's face, then shifted to her nephew. "No, sweetheart, it's still night. Go back to bed."

Toby gave David a curious look. "Who's that?" he demanded.

"This is Mr. Goddard, Toby. He's a friend of mine, a student in my cooking class."

Toby assessed David again. "You cook?" he wanted to know.

David laughed and the odd tension Holly had felt was broken. "Not very well, slugger," he retorted kindly, "but I'm learning."

"I'm not going to learn," Toby said firmly, drawing just a bit nearer to David, sensing, as Holly did, that this was a man who liked children.

"Oh, yeah? Why not?" David asked. And he sounded truly interested, not patronizing. "Don't you think men should cook?"

Toby shrugged, not exactly sure what he thought. "Mom cooks enough stuff. Do you think men should cook?"

David thought. "Yeah," he answered presently.

"Why?"

"Because they get hungry."

Toby grinned. "Wanna see my airplane?"

David looked to Holly for her permission; she liked him for doing that. She nodded.

"Sounds interesting," the man said to the boy, and then they were off to Toby's room to inspect the radio-controlled Cessna. The sound of their retreating voices gave Holly an odd feeling of well-being. Which was immediately spoiled by the ringing of the telephone.

She answered with a brisk and biting, "Yes?"

"Who is that Goddard guy?" Skyler demanded without preamble.

Holly drew a deep breath, then let it out again. Control, she must maintain her control. "David is a friend of mine, Skyler." Sugary acid slipped past her resolve, dripping from every word. "I am allowed to have friends, aren't I?"

"Not men!"

"Good night, Skyler," Holly sang, and then she set the receiver firmly back in its cradle.

Seconds later, the telephone rang again.

"Hello?" Holly said sweetly.

"Don't you ever hang up on me again, Holly Llewellyn!" Skyler shouted.

Of course, Holly had no choice but to do exactly that. She then switched on her answering machine, adjusting it to pick up on the first ring. If Skyler chose to call again, he would be cordially invited to leave his name, number and message. If he felt called upon to deliver a lecture, he would get only an electronic whirring sound in reply.

Holly was at the sink when David returned to the kitchen; though she didn't hear him, not consciously at least, she was aware of him in every sense. She stiffened as he came toward her, his boots making a melodic sound on the hard brick floor.

"Holly?"

She turned to face him. She couldn't keep her fingers from clenching the counter behind her.

David stopped, looking stricken. "You're afraid of me."

"Y-yes."

"Why?"

How could she explain, when she didn't understand it herself? She was afraid of David Goddard, and yet his nearness was causing every nerve-ending in her body to jump and crackle like naked electrical wire. Not even Ben—tender, laughing, lost Ben—had ever affected her in quite that way.

"Holly?" he prompted.

Holly felt very silly and not a little old-maidish. She blushed and gave a nervous, shaky laugh. "It's not as though I think you're...I mean...I know you're not—''

He was closer now. Holly could feel the heat and the strength of him. He was not yet touching her, but God help her, she wanted him to. She wanted him to hold her and kiss her and— He did. He kissed her. He cupped his gentle, strong hands, one on each side of her flushed face, bent his head, and kissed her. His lips were soft and cautious, making no demands.

A strange warmth filled Holly, stabbing her in some places, soothing her in others. She trembled when his tongue persuaded her lips to part for him and she moaned at his thorough, masterful yet entirely tender conquering.

And his body was warm and hard against Holly's, pressing, igniting licking flames of unfamiliar, unexpected passion. It hadn't been like this with Ben, she reflected frantically. Not even when they actually made love.

David drew back suddenly, with an obvious effort. "I'd better leave," he said in a hoarse voice, his eyes not quite linking with Holly's.

She was wounded and still breathless. "David—''

At last he looked at her, and she saw anguish in the depths of his eyes, along with a cold, self-directed anger. "I'm sorry," he rasped, reaching for his jacket.

Holly wanted to cry. She wanted to laugh. She didn't know what she wanted to do, except make love to David Goddard and have him make love to her. And that wasn't possible, of course, because they'd only known each other for a day and because Toby was sleeping upstairs. "Don't be sorry. You didn't do anything wrong."

"Didn't I?" he asked, speaking more to himself, it seemed, than to Holly.

Holly couldn't believe the crazy things that were going on inside her, the aching, melting sensations. The howling hunger. And her breasts. Her breasts quivered with a need to be fondled, their tips still at eager attention. What was happening to her?

"Will you come and have dinner with Toby and me tomorrow night, David?" she heard herself ask.

A log fell in the fireplace, sparks snapping. The silence was terrible and so was Holly's suspense. Which would be worse: his refusal or his acceptance?

"Yes," he said finally, and with some reluctance. "I know better, but I'll do it."

"Seven?" Holly asked with a calmness that amazed her. "We could go on to class afterward."

David wasn't looking at her; it seemed that he couldn't. The telephone jangled but the answering machine picked up instantly. The silence was heavy, pulsing.

"Seven," he said hoarsely, and then he was leaving, striding away from Holly with determined motions.

After she'd heard the front door close and the engine of his car start up with a fierce, revving sound, she could move again. She locked the house and turned out the few lights that still burned, then made her way upstairs.

Her bed looked as it always had—the same Pennsylvania Dutch quilt covered the practical flannel sheets beneath. The same brass headboard glistened in the light from the lamp on her dresser. The same two pillows waited, neither having ever borne the weight of a man's head. Not Skyler's certainly. Not even Ben's.

The bed was unchanged, but Holly's feelings about sharing it were vastly different. Tonight it looked lonely and cold rather than spacious.

Shaking her head, she went into the small bathroom adjoining her room, washed her face, brushed her teeth, stripped off the black slacks and red sweater she had worn that night, and finally the wispy panties and bra underneath.

Holly stood naked before the full-length mirror on the back of her bedroom door. She saw a well-proportioned if unremarkable body, curved in some places, hollowed in others.

She permitted herself to remember that long-ago summer, between high school and college, when she and Ben had given in to the dizzying, constant demands of their youthful bodies. She had not soared, as books and movies had led her to believe she would, but she had not been traumatized, either. Ben's lovemaking had been gentle and pleasant, if not truly fulfilling.

But now, as the result of one brief kiss, Holly knew that, with David Goddard, her body would respond with abandon. It would sing. It would quiver.

The prospect was completely alarming.

With flouncing motions, Holly stormed over to her dresser, wrenched open a drawer and pulled out a long T-shirt style gown. She quickly put the garment on, as though that would dispel the crazy hungers, the yearnings, that had lain dormant until one particular man had kissed her.

Determinedly, she got into bed and settled into the warmth of the soft flannel sheets. Unable to sleep, she tossed this way and that, plumping her pillows, lying down and sitting back up again.

After almost twenty minutes of this, Holly faced a very disturbing fact. Sure as the sun would rise in the morning, sure as the December snows would fall, David Goddard was going to make love to her. It was inevitable; it was inescapable. The self-control she needed in order to feel strong and safe would desert her.

Tears burned in Holly's eyes and flowed down her cheeks. She would be changed forever and then she would be left because David was not what he seemed to be, not what he claimed to be.

All her instincts warned that this was true and yet she could feel herself sliding toward him, careening down some steep psychological hill. And there was nothing to grasp, nothing to break her fall.

She rolled over and sniffled, tucking both hands under her face the way she had as a little girl. Skyler. She would think of Skyler and everything would be all right.

What did Skyler look like? She couldn't remember. After dating the man for months, she couldn't remember!

"Oh, damn!" Holly cried into the quilt edge that was bunched in her hands. Again she tried to summon Skyler's face to her mind but it wouldn't come; instead, she saw David's dark hair, David's strong jawline, David's ferociously blue eyes.

"Who are you, David Goddard?" Holly wailed inwardly, her mind full of shimmering tangles of fear and joy, happiness and dread. Who are you?

Except for the wild, thunderous beating of her own heart, there was no answer.

## Chapter Four

Wearing his favorite blue running suit, David bent and tapped the side of the glass fishbowl with an impatient index finger. The two goldfish floated, one above the other, just staring at him, their shimmering fan-shaped tails barely moving.

"You guys are really boring, you know that?" he complained in an undertone. "I bought you to give this place some color and flash and what do you do? You just sit there, watching the world go by. Swim, dammit!"

The fish regarded him implacably, still hovering midway between the surface of the water and the bottom, with its blue rocks and shifting plastic fern and dime-store diver.

"No class," David grumbled, turning away and wrenching the damp sweatband from his forehead in one irritated movement.

Still breathing hard from his customary morning run, he stumbled into the bathroom and took a quick shower. Later, as he dried himself and dressed—in the living room, for God's sake—he wondered how the hell he was ever going to impress Holly Llewellyn with a place like this.

Draping a towel over his shoulders because his hair was still dripping wet, he took in the goldfish, the unmade sofa bed, the spots on the carpet. No class. Like those seventy-nine-cent goldfish, the place had no class.

The telephone rang and David, who had been indulging in a fanciful nostalgia for his real apartment in faraway Georgetown, was startled. He put images of good art, the hot-tub in his bathroom and the ivory fireplace out of his mind as he lunged for the instrument.

"Goddard," he answered, and the long-distance buzz coming over the wire told him that he'd been right. This was his call from Washington.

"Zigman here," Walt replied. "The Bureau staked out the address in L.A., Goddard, but they must have muffed it somehow, because Llewellyn didn't bite."

David had a headache. He had hoped the FBI would be able to collar Llewellyn immediately; like a child about to have a sliver pulled, he'd wanted the whole thing to be over with. "He was an agent himself once. He probably knows the signs."

"Yeah."

"Does this mean I can drop the case and come back to Washington?" Part of David hoped it did, while another part wanted to watch Holly Llewellyn forever.

"Hell, no. The little lady sent him a letter, didn't she? You saw it with your own eyes, Goddard. That means she's in fairly regular contact with our boy, doesn't it?''

David resented the "little lady" reference. Holly was so much more and the phrase seemed to demean her. "Holly is a woman, Walt. With a brain."

Zigman's laugh traveled three thousand miles to annoy David as instantly as if he'd been in the same room. "Goddard, you are going soft. Don't get to liking this broad too much. She's in line for an indictment herself, you know."

"For what?" David snapped.

"Christ," Zigman swore impatiently. "For aiding and abetting a fugitive. Are you going to wake the hell up, Goddard, or do I have to send somebody else out there to handle this thing?"

David bit back all the fury that surged like bile into his throat. He'd never been pulled from a detail in all the time he'd worked for the service, and he wasn't about to start now. Besides, he couldn't be sure how another agent would manage the situation. And it was delicate. Holly's emotional state was delicate. "I can handle it," he said.

"Wouldn't have sent you if I didn't think you could," Walt replied in smug tones. His cigar stub was probably bobbing up and down in his mouth, and David wished he could be there to squash it into the man's teeth. "Keep a sharp eye out, Goddard. Llewellyn could turn up there. If he does, I want him busted. On the spot."

The thought made David half sick, and he closed his eyes. His wet hair was dripping cold trails down his neck and he began drying it with one end of the towel. He could imagine the look on Holly's face if he casually wrestled Llewellyn to the floor in her living room. "Yeah."

"Can you handle him by yourself or do you want a detail? The Bureau has an office in Spokane—"

"You keep the Bureau the hell out of this, Walt! I mean it!" The outburst was too sudden, too emotional. David drew a deep breath and stopped toweling his hair to sigh. "Llewellyn is a former agent," he reiterated a moment later, when he could speak more moderately. "If he sees a bunch of three-piece suits and crew cuts watching his sister's house, how do you think he'll react?"

"He'll split, just like he did in L.A."

"Right." David sighed again, running one hand through his hair. "Let me handle this, will you, Walt? If I need the Bureau, I can always call them in."

"All right," Walt agreed in his gruff, wry way. "But you remember why you're there. It isn't to make fruitcake, Goddard. Or time."

David's headache was infinitely worse. "Yeah," he agreed after a long, long time. "I'll remember."

"Good," came the brisk reply. "When do you see the broad again?"

Enough was enough. He'd let that word pass once; he couldn't do it again. "Don't call her that again, Walt. If you do, your nose will be where your right ear is now. I'll see to it."

Zigman swore and rang off.

David held the receiver in his hand for a long time, doing some swearing of his own. Craig Llewellyn was going to show up in Spokane, he could feel it in his bones. It was only a matter of time. Holly was going to be destroyed by the inevitable arrest, by David's deception.

Why the hell had he accepted the dinner invitation, dammit? Suppose there was a replay of that episode when he'd kissed her, in the kitchen? What then? David had spent most of the night reliving that ill-guided indulgence and imagining all the sweet pleasures that could have come after it.

He shook his head, trying to dislodge the thought, but his body recollected perfectly. Heatedly. He'd had his share of women, of course, but none had ever made him feel quite the way Holly did. She could reach past the hard finish painted over him by his Secret Service training. She could so easily reach past it.

Maybe Walt Zigman was right; maybe he was losing his ability to be objective. Maybe he was getting soft.

David allowed himself one rueful, humorless chuckle. Soft was definitely not the word. Not where Holly Llewellyn was concerned.

The day was a full and busy one, but it took forever to pass, all the same. Instead of thinking about her newspaper column, as she should have been, every turn of Holly's mind seemed to lead to David Goddard.

Elaine was gathering together the leaves of the manuscript she had been working on, preparing to leave. "What time is the hunk coming over?" she asked.

Color leaped into Holly's cheeks and pounded there. "What hunk?" she asked tightly, a little annoyed that Elaine could read her preoccupation so easily.

"Don't give me that. I'm talking about your date with David Goddard and you know it. What are you serving? What are you wearing? Do you want me to take Toby home with me for the evening?''

"Once your questions start coming, there's no stopping them, is there?" Holly countered, still flushed. She took the disk containing her pitiful effort at a cooking column from the computer and shut off the machine with an angry flourish.

Elaine was not intimidated, but she did back off just a little. "I could take Toby home," she offered again. "Roy and I enjoy him so much, and—"

"Toby is staying right here!"

"Why? Do you need him as a buffer, Holly?"

Holly had been halfway out of her chair; now she sagged back into it. "I wouldn't use Toby that way, Elaine," she said, but the doubt in her voice bothered her.

"It's all right, you know, to want time alone with an attractive man. It's not going to scar Toby's pysche or anything."

In spite of herself, Holly chuckled. Elaine did have a way of lightening a situation. "Last night," she confessed after a few moments of reflection, "David kissed me."

"So?"

"So it was weird, Elaine. The earth moved. Bells chimed. All the corny stuff you see in movies and read about in books—it all happened."

Elaine beamed. "That's great!"

"It is not," Holly insisted, her face set and serious again. "It's terrible. That man is dangerous, Elaine."

"Dangerous? Why?"

Now Holly felt foolish and she couldn't quite bring herself to meet her friend's eyes. "He's not like Skyler. He's—"

"Thank God for small favors."

Holly was putting her computer disk into its paper folder, covering the terminal, clearing her desk. Anything to keep from looking directly at Elaine. "You don't like Skyler, do you? I can understand why Toby doesn't, but you should."

"He's all right," Elaine conceded with a heavy and somewhat dramatic sigh. "It's just that he's so, well, you know, safe. Boring."

"He's reliable, that's what he is," defended Holly. "I might marry him."

"If you do, you're crazy. You don't love Skyler, Holly."

"How do you know?" Holly demanded. But she wished with all her heart that she could love Skyler, truly want him. Even need him. It made her mad that she couldn't.

"If you loved him, ninny-brain, you wouldn't be all hot and bothered because David Goddard is coming to dinner. You haven't thought straight all day."

Holly slumped. "I'm not 'hot and bothered'!" she lied in a plaintive wail.

Elaine only laughed. "Let me take Toby home with me. Please? I promise to give him the most nutritionally balanced TV dinner in the freezer, and I'll bring him home after your class lets out."

Holly hadn't even thought about the class. Dear Lord, that was one more thing to add to the worries she already had, like what she was going to serve David Goddard for dinner and what she was going to wear. She wanted to look attractive, but not predatory....

It was as though, by their long and friendly association, Elaine had learned to look right inside Holly's brain and read her every thought. "Wear something sexy. Leopard skin, maybe."

Holly laughed. "Leopard skin? This is a quiet, casual dinner, not a movie about barbarians! And I have no desire to look 'sexy.'"

"Pity," Elaine said, looking entirely serious. "A woman ought to wear something sort of Frederick's-of-Hollywoodish once in a while."

Holly only shook her head, amazed. She wanted to ask if Elaine herself ever wore such garments but didn't quite dare.

"Hey, Tobe!" Elaine yelled, shaking off the look of deep thought, beaming again. "Come on! You're coming home with me tonight!"

The TV, blaring in the family room, went silent. The next sound, in fact, was a little boy's whoop of delight. Toby bounded into the room, already struggling into his jacket, his face shining. "Do you think Uncle Roy will play Donkey Kong with me?"

Elaine gave the child a conspiratorial smile. "Yes. But you must promise to let him beat you at least once."

Toby squared his small shoulders manfully and looked charitably reluctant. "Oh, all right. But just once."

There was a whoosh of good-byes, Toby planting a quick, wet kiss on Holly's cheek, and then a swirl of cold air when the back door was opened. And they were gone.

Holly sighed, and as an aching sense of loneliness grasped her, she took herself firmly in hand. "Frederick's of Hollywood!" she muttered irritably as she went to the freezer to take out fried rice and egg rolls, experiments from last week's chapter of her new cookbook.

She slammed the foil-wrapped packages down on the counter top, near the sink. If David Goddard didn't like eating experiments, the heck with him. What did he think this place was, a restaurant? Why, if he said one single word, she would...she would...

Holly sighed. Who was she kidding? She put the egg rolls and fried rice back into the freezer and took out the special beef stroganoff she'd been saving in case Skyler's parents decided to come to Spokane on one of their infrequent visits.

After straightening the kitchen and throwing together a green salad, she raced upstairs to take a shower and exchange her jeans and madras shirt for something more—more what? Sexy?

Still dripping from her shower, wrapped only in a bright pink bath sheet, Holly shoved the white cashmere jumpsuit back into the closet. It was too clingy, that was all. Entirely too clingy.

She brought out a flowing blue caftan, interwoven with tiny silver threads, that she'd picked up in Hong Kong only the month before. Even then she'd had no idea where she would wear such a thing, but she hadn't been able to resist the gown's quiet elegance.

She returned that garment to the closet, too. After all, it had that deep neckline and it was too formal. Whatever she chose would have to do for the cooking class she had to teach after dinner, she reminded herself.

Finally, Holly settled for tailored black slacks and a soft mulberry sweater. Not exactly suited to making Belgian fruitcake, she thought, but at least she would look halfway decent when David arrived and she could always push up the sleeves later, when it was time to conduct her class.

Hurriedly, she brushed her hair, applied her makeup and brushed her hair again. She allowed herself one cool misting of the expensive perfume she'd once bought on a dash through the Paris airport.

When the rites of womanhood had all been performed, she stood back from the mirror to look at herself. Her lipstick was crooked, and she wiped it off and re-applied it, this time using a lip liner. "Color inside the lines, now," she mocked herself.

David arrived promptly at seven o'clock, just as they'd agreed. Not a moment before and not a moment after. Something about this small precision bothered Holly, but she pushed the feeling aside.

There was a fire crackling in the living-room fireplace and the table in the rarely used dining room had been set with pretty china and her grandmother's silver. David looked impossibly handsome in his gray slacks, creamy-white sweater, and navy-blue jacket. No indeed, this was no time for silly doubts.

"Come in," she said, stepping back.

David smiled, but the look in his eyes was weary. Perhaps he'd had a hard day at law school. He extended a bottle of wine and then took off his coat. "Where's Toby?" he asked, and the expression in his indigo-blue eyes was suddenly expectant.

Holly was a bit embarrassed. Now she was going to have to say that Toby was spending the evening at Elaine and Roy's, and it would look as though she'd been setting the scene for a steamy seduction. Why, oh, why had she lighted the fire and set the table so carefully? "He had a previous engagement," she said.

"Good," David replied smoothly.

"Good?" Holly echoed, confused.

David laughed. "A man's got to have a social life," he answered, and Holly remained off-balance because she didn't know whether he meant that Toby needed a social life or he did.

They ate in the dining room, with the candles lit— Holly had been too shy to light them, so David had done it—with the wine and the good china and the glint of the aged silver flatware. Holly hadn't entertained a man in this particular way in as long as she could remember, and she was uncomfortable and distracted, not knowing what to do or how to act. The fact that she silently flogged herself for being silly didn't help; she still felt like a fifteen-year-old about to go to her first prom.

"Do we have time to sit by the fire for a while," David asked easily, setting his wineglass aside, "or are we off to tackle the mysteries of Belgian rum sauce?"

Holly laughed, even though the thought of sitting in front of a romantic winter fire with a man—with *this* man—patently made her nervous. "We have a few minutes."

He stood up, but instead of coming around to pull back Holly's chair, as Skyler would have done, he started gathering up dirty dishes. Holly was disappointed for a moment, but then she decided that one act was as considerate as the other and began to help.

Holly waited, every nerve screaming, for him to kiss her. He didn't do it while they were clearing the table, of course, and in the kitchen he kept the dishwasher door between them as they put the china and silverware inside. Was he shy or something?

Holly's cheeks stung with color. Elaine was right, she castigated herself angrily, you're hot and bothered!

Once the dishwasher was churning away, David caught Holly's hand casually in his and led her back to the living room as though it were his house. As though they had all the time in the world.

"Maybe we shouldn't—" she sputtered, lifting his hand so that she could peer at the watch on her own wrist. "It's getting late—"

David sat down on one of the soft Indian pillows facing the fireplace and pulled Holly after him. She tumbled against him, and her heart lurched into her throat at even that small contact, driving the breath out of her lungs and causing a curious ringing sound in her ears.

She settled herself primly on the other pillow, careful not to look at him. She knew that she would see the familiar, quiet amusement shining in his navy-blue eyes.

"Holly."

She swallowed, knotting her hands together in her lap. "What?"

"Look at me."

She looked at him because doing otherwise would have been foolish and petulant. Even infantile. "So, I'm looking already," she said.

He laughed and that was at variance with the look in his eyes which, instead of humor, betrayed a reluctance of some kind. A hurtful reluctance.

Holly was stung. David wanted to resist her as badly as she wanted to resist him! Wasn't she attractive? Did he find her—David bent his head and kissed her, and an almost inaudible groan rumbled up through his

chest and brushed against her lips. He was only nibbling at her mouth, tasting it as though it were a deli-
cacy to be savored. He muttered something, and to a
dazed Holly, it sounded as though he'd said, "Why?"

She couldn't think of that now. She couldn't think
of anything except the havoc that reluctant kiss was
causing inside her. She shivered and placed her hands
on his strong shoulders, where they moved of their
own accord to caress his neck.

He kissed her in earnest then, his tongue exploring
the sweet depths of her mouth, enlisting her own to
respond in quick, fevered parries. His hand moving
gently up and down the length of her thigh caused the
flesh hidden beneath to quiver.

Holly wanted to die and she wanted to live forever.
She wanted to stop and she drew him nearer, allowing
him to shift her body and his own so that they were
both prone before the crackling fire.

His hand left her thigh to move up over her hip,
underneath her soft mulberry sweater, over the flesh
at her waist, over her rib cage. He freed her from his
sorcerer's kiss to nibble gently, provocatively, at her
earlobe and her neck.

"I want you, Holly," he said in that forthright way
of his, his voice a gruff caress against the base of her
neck.

Holly shivered, even though there was a heat pulsing inside her that made her long to fling off her
clothes. "David, I...we..."

"I know," he chuckled, and his hand had found the
catch at the front of her bra. There was a feeling of
sweet, wanton freedom as her breasts were released,
and then his fingers were soothing her, searching out

a nipple that already awaited them at strictest attention. "Tell me to stop."

If Holly hadn't been so bedazzled, she would have slapped him. "I can't..." she admitted, her words falling away to a groan as he found that arching nipple and rolled it gently between his fingers.

He drew her sweater slowly upward, his hand cupping the captured breast, shaping it for conquering. When he bent his head to lave the throbbing peak softly with his tongue, Holly gasped with pleasure and arched her back in reflexive surrender.

"We...can't do this..." he managed to say as his mouth blazed a path from the conquered breast to the one that awaited sweet defeat. "We can't..."

"I know," Holly agreed. But when his tongue touched the untended nipple, she knotted her hands in David's rich, mink-soft hair and held him close.

Holly Llewellyn was to wonder many times, sometimes with regret and sometimes with relief, what would have happened if the telephone hadn't rung when it did. Its cold, jarring jangle made David thrust himself away from her as if in fury.

Stung and shaken and still needing, Holly hastily fixed her bra and stumbled off at a half jog to answer.

"Hello!" she gasped, winded and embarrassed. She could see David from where she stood and he was just staring into the fire, his broad back rigid.

"Sis?"

Holly wanted to cry. Not now, she thought frantically. Oh, God, not now! She lowered her voice. "Hello, Craig."

"'Hello, Craig'? Is that all you've got to say?"

Holly stiffened, very conscious of the man sitting before the fireplace. Her breasts were still heavy and warm with passion, their peaks moist. She tried to breathe properly. "What should I say, Craig?" she asked petulantly, forgetting this time to keep her tone at whisper level.

"I tried to pick up the money," Craig rushed on angrily, frantically. "Guess what? There were crew cuts all around Cindy's place!"

Holly trembled, then drew a deep breath. "Crew cuts?" she repeated, confused. David's back stiffened almost imperceptibly, or was that a trick of the firelight? He didn't appear to be making the slightest effort to hear what was being said, but appearances could be deceiving.

"FBI agents. Holly, they were everywhere! Did you turn me in?"

"Of course I didn't!" At this outburst, David turned his head, assessing Holly with a look she could read all too well: it was full of stark, angry pity.

"Just listen," Craig rasped. God in heaven, how desperate, how hunted, he sounded. "I'm going to need money, Holly, and if I have to come there and get it, I will!"

"You can't do that! Toby would be—"

"Toby. Always Toby. Don't you ever think about anybody besides that kid, Holly? What about me? I'm your brother, remember?" Craig stopped to draw a harsh breath and then began to cough. It was a frightening sound.

"You're sick!" Holly exclaimed, watching David. He had turned his eyes from her again and was now gazing into the fire, one knee drawn up under his chin. "Craig, please—turn yourself in. They won't hurt you, I swear it!"

"I'll call again tomorrow!" Craig roared impatiently, and then he slammed the receiver down so hard that Holly flinched. She was on the verge of tears when she placed her own receiver in its cradle.

The silence in the living room was complete, except for the snapping merriment of the fire. David looked at Holly but did not rise from his seat near the hearth. Holly closed her eyes momentarily, in a vain effort to shut out the reality of Craig and his problems, then drew a deep breath to steady herself.

"Y-you're a lawyer," she began, speaking as casually as she could. "If someone is wanted by the law, and another person...a person close to them...knows where they are and sometimes gives them money..."

David rose slowly to his feet with the grace of a predatory animal, but he kept his distance. And it was more than a physical distance. "Then that person is guilty of aiding and abetting a fugitive," he said evenly. "They could, under some circumstances, be imprisoned."

Holly trembled and bit her lower lip. When she closed her eyes against the possibility, her already precarious balance was affected and she swayed. David was instantly clasping her shoulders, holding her upright. And while there was a gentleness in his touch, there was little sympathy.

"I can help you, Holly," he said hoarsely. "If you'll just allow yourself to trust me, I swear I can help you."

Holly longed to pour out the whole ugly story, to tell him how scared and confused Craig was, to explain that he hadn't meant to do all those awful things. But she didn't dare. The fact that she had almost given herself to David moments before, making a joyous offering of something she held dear, changed nothing.

David Goddard was still a stranger.

## Chapter Five

The rest of that week was dismal for Holly. She couldn't concentrate on her work and she was short not only with Elaine but with Toby. When Skyler called, offering an innocent-sounding invitation to lunch, she all but bit his head off.

In the evenings, of course, she taught her cooking class, and David was always there, always attentive—and never friendly. He might have been a total stranger, answering what casual questions Holly could contrive to ask with flat, clipped banalities. Not once did he stay to help with the cleanup, as he had those first two nights, and he certainly made no effort to contact her outside of class.

Holly was devastated and she was scared, too. Craig had nearly been caught in Los Angeles. How could the FBI have known where he would be if not for David's seeing the address on that letter she'd mailed? And that night, that shattering night when they had almost made love, David had said, *"I can help you, Holly. If you'll just allow yourself to trust me. I swear I can help you."*

He knew; she was sure he knew. And as far as Holly was concerned, that was reason enough not to see him again. Ever.

Except that she needed him, wanted him. Perhaps, though she couldn't often bring herself to examine the possibility rationally, she even loved David Goddard.

On Friday night, Skyler called to ask her out for dinner and a movie. Holly refused, pleading a headache, and went to bed early, setting the answering machine because Skyler had a tendency to be persistent. The telephone rang twice during the night, and a sleepless Holly timed the calls at eleven-thirty-five and twelve-ten.

The next morning was one of those springlike days that sometimes creep into winter. Though there were still ragged patches of snow on the ground, the sun was bright and the sky was a painfully keen shade of blue.

The weather did much to bring Holly out of her doldrums, and to make up for some of the stresses of the past week, she suggested to a rather wan and distraught Toby that they take his airplane to Manito Park and fly it.

"I'm going to the Ice Capades this afternoon," Toby reminded his aunt, running his spoon glumly through the dish of oatmeal before him. "My whole class is going."

"I remember," Holly said softly. It hurt, this restraint between herself and Toby. It was a sad, pulsing ache. "You'll be back in plenty of time, I promise."

Toby brightened. "Okay," he chirped. "Let's hurry up with breakfast and go!"

His ebullience made Holly laugh, easing the bereft feeling inside her. "Let's do that. Be sure to wear your mittens because it's cold."

Toby nodded. As he passed Holly's desk, his oatmeal gleefully abandoned on the trestle table, he stopped. "Mom, there's messages on the machine. The light is flashing."

Holly glanced uneasily toward the telephone. Between Craig and Skyler, it was getting so that she didn't like to answer the thing at all. It wasn't likely that David had left those messages, she told herself, and she was in no mood to hear a lecture from Skyler or a lot of pathos from Craig. "I'll listen later. Right now, I'm in the mood to fly your Cessna."

"Me, too!" Toby agreed, and he was off again, in search of the warmer clothes he would need for a morning in the park.

Perhaps too conscientious for her own good, Holly went to the telephone answering machine and frowned down at the little red light blinking so industriously, her finger poised over the "play" button. What if the calls had been from Craig and he was in terrible trouble? What if— She stopped herself, sighed and drew back her hand. It could wait. Whatever it was, it could just wait. Any kind of hassle at this moment would be too much.

The park was sunny, and in places patches of green-brown grass dappled the grubby snow. There were lots of children around, their laughter ringing in the ice-cold air, and a goodly number of parents, too.

"I wish I'd brought my sled," Toby said wistfully, watching as some of the children pushed and pulled each other on Flyers and plastic saucers.

Something twisted inside Holly as she watched her nephew; despite all his friends at school, he was a lonely child, often feeling separate from the others. Alone. While Holly's own childhood had been far from ideal, she had had Craig. Toby had no one near his own age.

The little boy squinted up at her, a grin forming on his face, and the toy Cessna seemed huge in his small hands. "You thinkin' about my dad?" he asked directly.

Holly was stunned. Lately it seemed as though she went around with all her thoughts written on her forehead, so clearly did people read them. "How did you know that?"

Small shoulders, hidden beneath the weight of a down-filled snowsuit, moved in a shrug. "You get a sad look on your face when you think about Dad."

"We were very close once," Holly admitted distractedly, having to look away for a moment because of the tears that stung her eyes.

"Dad's a bad man, isn't he?" Toby probed seriously, his mittened hands working awkwardly with the airplane.

Holly shook her head so suddenly and so hard that her neck ached—as did her heart. "No, Toby. Your dad isn't really a bad man, though he has done some bad things. He's sick, Toby, and pretty confused."

"He doesn't want me."

Holly knelt in the snow, which crackled beneath the worn knees of her oldest jeans, and clasped Toby by the shoulders. "It isn't that way at all, Toby. Your dad loves you. But when people have the kind of troubles he does, they just don't seem to have room in their lives for other things and other people.''

Toby's face was scrunched up in the battle against unmanly emotion. ''I liked Mr. Goddard a lot. How come he didn't come back? Does he have problems, too, like Dad?''

Holly closed her eyes for a moment and drew a deep breath. ''No, Toby. I don't think he has the kind of problems that your dad has. As for why he didn't come back—''

''He was a fool,'' put in a deep, masculine voice.

Holly and Toby looked up simultaneously, squinting against the dazzling winter sun, to see David standing over them. He wore a dark-blue ski jacket and jeans, a contrite expression on his face and held his own model airplane in his hands.

''Hi!'' Toby whooped, overjoyed.

While Holly was glad enough to see David herself, glad enough to shout, in fact, she was a little injured by Toby's enthusiasm toward the man. It was as though a hopeless day had just been saved at the last, cliff-hanging second. And there were all her misgivings, too...

''Truce,'' he said gruffly, extending one hand to Holly, the plane tucked under his opposite elbow now. ''Please?''

Holly swallowed. It was sheer, foolhardy madness to get further involved with this man and she knew it, but she couldn't quite bring herself to refuse what she knew he was offering. ''Truce,'' she croaked out, after what seemed like a long time.

Eyes of an impossibly dark blue swept over her so swiftly that she could almost believe it hadn't happened, and then they shifted to Toby. "Hi, slugger. Ready to fly?"

Toby was literally beaming. Again Holly found his obvious fondness for David Goddard unsettling. What would happen when David went away? What if he did something that would hurt Craig and thus Toby, too?

"I'm ready!" came the exuberant answer.

David proved to be a lousy pilot, always dropping his hand-controls or sending his somewhat odd-looking model airplane plunging into bushes, but Holly was too amused to chalk this up as another reason to be suspicious of him. After all, he'd only said he owned a model plane, not that he was proficient at flying one.

In any case, David's ineptitude only seemed to endear him further to Toby, who patiently demonstrated again and again how to handle the craft properly. Holly stood back and watched, full of mingled dread and tender inclinations. She was glad, even relieved, when Toby offered her a turn with his airplane, for that gave her something to think about besides David Goddard and all the wonderful, terrible things that could come of allowing him into her life.

As the small airplane glided and dipped and roared overhead in a perfect circle, following the radar commands Holly gave it with her handset, Toby and David both applauded. Privately, she was surprised that she hadn't sent the thing crashing into a tree; her fingers wouldn't stop shaking.

Finally the morning ended; it was time to take Toby home, give him lunch and let him have a few quiet minutes before driving him to the Coliseum, where he would join his classmates for the afternoon performance of the Ice Capades.

Leading Toby toward her car, she glanced uncertainly at David. What would happen now? Did he want to talk? Would he just leave, or would there be a renewal of the dangerous attraction that seemed to be sweeping them together?

Holly felt stiff, almost formal. Walk away and don't look back! screamed her mind. This man is dangerous! But her heart said something entirely different. "We enjoyed seeing you again," she ventured aloud.

David's lips curved into a half grin, one that said he understood her feelings because they so closely paralleled his own, but his blue eyes were sad. "Toby will be busy this afternoon?" he asked evenly.

"I'm going to the Ice Capades!" the little boy crowed before Holly could assemble a polite answer.

David's indigo gaze touched the child with real affection, then sliced back to Holly's face. "I need to talk with you, Holly," he said quietly. "To be with you. Will you have lunch with me?"

"Sure she will!" Toby announced with loud confidence, scrambling into the backseat of Holly's car, setting his airplane and handset on the seat and buckling himself into the seat belt.

David laughed, but that quiet ache was still visible in his eyes. "Please," he said.

Holly swallowed hard and nodded. "Shall I meet you somewhere?"

"I'll pick you up at your place in an hour or so, if that's all right."

Holly nodded again and got into her car, busying herself with the fastening of her seat belt and the turning of the ignition key. Anything so that she didn't have to look back and see David getting into that rented car of his, that car that didn't suit him. She couldn't bear the strain of wondering about him anymore, of weighing his motives all the time. No, just for this one day she was going to enjoy what she felt, without letting doubt spoil it.

While Toby consumed soup and a sandwich, his appetite made sharp by a morning of fresh air and exercise, Holly exchanged her Saturday jeans for a pair of fitted gray slacks, her T-shirt and poncho for a classic navy-blue blouse with a tie at the throat and a charcoal velvet blazer. She brushed her hair carefully and put on makeup, too, telling herself all the while that she wasn't trying to be attractive for David, not at all. It was just that as something of a local celebrity, she had an image to maintain.

Why she hadn't been concerned with that image earlier in the day, when she'd gone to a public park in her oldest clothes, wearing no makeup, was a question she didn't bother to examine.

When she returned from dropping Toby off at the Coliseum, David was waiting in front of her house. And he was driving a different car.

Holly parked her own Toyota in the driveway, locked it and went toward him, taking in the sleek lines of the red Camaro sitting at the curb. David got out, looking devastatingly handsome in jeans and a cream-colored bulky-knit sweater, and came around to open the car door for her.

"What happened to the rented one?" she asked. "The brown sedan?"

David shook his head, but he went back around the car and got in on his own side before answering. "I told you my car was being fixed, Holly. This is it."

Again, Holly was unsettled. This car looked and smelled so new, how could anything have been wrong with it?

"Don't weigh everything I say, Holly," David said watching her. "I'm a man, not a mystery to solve."

Holly said nothing. She couldn't deny that he was a man, but the part about his not being a mystery was certainly open to debate.

Lunch, eaten in a plant-filled restaurant overlooking Riverfront Park, the site of a world's fair and Spokane's coveted antique carousel, was a stilted affair.

Holly was as annoyed as she was self-conscious. Hadn't David said he wanted to talk to her? No, in fact, he'd said he *needed* to talk to her. So why didn't he?

His glass of white wine seemed to fascinate him; he turned it in one strong, sun-browned hand, watching the ebb and flow. The silence lengthened.

"I thought you said we were going to talk!" Holly blurted out impatiently. What was it about this man that undid her so? She felt sure that it was more than her rising attraction to him, more even than her doubts about his motives for spending time with her.

He chuckled and the sound was hollow and humorless. "You're in a lot of trouble, aren't you, Holly? Or, I should say, someone very close to you is. Why won't you let me help you?"

Holly bit her lower lip. She wasn't about to make any admissions about Craig and her involvement in his many troubles, but she wanted to. She wanted to let everything pour out. "I don't need any help and I'm not in trouble," she said stubbornly when David's indigo eyes impaled her with an unspoken challenge. "What gave you that idea?"

He made an exasperated sound. "I'm not an idiot, Holly. I was there when this person called, whoever they are."

If Holly felt alarm, she also felt a paradoxical sort of comfort. Could it be that, for all her imaginings, David really didn't know that her caller was Craig? "I think we should leave," she said stiffly.

"Fine," David replied, setting his wineglass down with a jarring thump and rising from his chair to draw back Holly's.

The flesh on the back of her neck tingled as it was brushed briefly by the hard wall of his midsection. Even that small contact stirred the melting warmth deep in Holly's middle and made her heart beat at a faster pace.

She was still shivering when they reached his car.

"Take me home, please," she said, struggling not to fling herself into his arms like some helpless bit of fluff and sob out all the things that were tormenting her.

"Don't worry," he replied in a terse whisper.

But, at the house, he lingered. Against her better judgment, Holly invited him inside for coffee. Just passing through the living room, where they had so nearly made love the night Craig called and ruined everything, made Holly's face burn.

She was grateful to reach the cookbook-cluttered, sensible kitchen. What could happen here?

Too late, Holly remembered the first soul-jarring kiss. That was what could happen here.

She busied herself with the coffee maker, filling the decanter with cold water, putting a new filter and fresh grounds into the basket. She was so very much on guard that her shoulders ached.

"Holly."

She stiffened as she felt David approach, but could not bring herself to turn around and face him. His hands closed over her shoulders and began gently working the taut muscles there.

"Scary, isn't it?" he asked in a low voice, his breath brushing Holly's ear and part of her cheek.

"Wh-what?" Holly hedged. She knew she should break out of David's hold, but she didn't have the spirit to do that. Besides, the massage he was giving her felt so good.

"The way we need each other."

Holly lifted her chin, barely able to keep from letting her head roll as the muscles in her shoulders were forced to relax. "I don't want to need anybody," she managed to say.

"Neither do I," came the prompt, gruff reply. "But there it is."

He was close, the length of his body comfortingly hard and strong against Holly. Suddenly his hands stopped working her shoulders to cup her breasts with a bold gentleness that caused her to draw in a swift, audible breath.

"D-David—"

His thumbs were stroking her nipples through the thin fabric of her blouse and the gossamer bra beneath. "Let me make love to you, Holly," he said hoarsely, his lips now touching the outer rim of her ear and making every part of her leap with a stinging desire. "If we don't, I'm going to go crazy."

Holly trembled, her head falling backward to press into David's broad shoulder, her eyes closed. "At least you're still sane," she admitted, breathless. "I'm already over the edge. I must be, to do this..."

The delicious torment of her breasts stopped; he turned her swiftly to face him. And new torments, even sweeter than those that had gone before, took over as he kissed her. Holly's knees quivered, threatening to give out, and David supported her by pressing closer, fairly pinning her to the counter's edge.

When he drew back, he searched her face with that same broken, needing look in his eyes. "Holly?"

Flushed, Holly nodded, and that was answer enough for David. He lifted her up into his arms and, at her direction, mumbled into his neck, carried her upstairs and into the bedroom. There, he dropped her summarily onto the rumpled covers, and she had cause to be embarrassed again because she had forgotten to make the bed.

To hide that, she tried to make a joke. "You boldly go where no man has gone before, I'll say that for you."

The indigo gaze impaled her. "Are you saying that you've never..."

Hastily, coloring again, Holly shook her head. "No. My...my fiancé—"

He sat down on the bed beside her, his fingers woven together, hands dangling between his knees. "It's all right, Holly. Just tell me one thing: is this really what you want? If it isn't, I'll leave right now and we'll pretend that none of it ever happened."

Holly did not want David to go. She wanted him to hold her, kiss her, love her. But she couldn't say any of those things because her throat was constricted.

David must have read her need in her eyes and in the flush on her cheekbones, for he kicked off his polished boots and stretched out on the bed beside Holly, wrapping one arm around her, holding her close. She loved the clean scent of his hair and skin, the tender threat of his powerful body.

Eventually he kissed her again, tentatively at first, as though he expected her to push him away. When she didn't, the kiss deepened and with his free hand he began to caress her, cupping the other at the back of her head. After a very long time, she felt crooned in sleepy surrender, arching her back just slightly in acquiescence.

When the blouse had been opened completely and laid aside, David unfastened her bra. Her breasts moved with voluptuous freedom, the peaks tightening in response to the fate that awaited them and the coolness of the air.

David continued to caress her, brushing the wanton nipples with his fingertips, charting the rows of her ribs, circling her naval. And all the while, he kissed her, seeking every depth and secret, consuming even as he cherished.

After a time, he kissed the line of her jaw, sampled her earlobe, traced a path of fire down the white length of her neck. When he found her breast and took the nipple full in his mouth to suckle, Holly arched her back again, electrified, and gasped out a senseless cry of welcome.

Meanwhile, his hand undid the tricky buckle on her belt, the button of her slacks and the zipper. Holly felt the fabric of both the slacks and her panties sliding downward and gloried in the sensation.

David left the sensuous warmth of her breasts to brush his lips down the length of her rib cage, first on one side and then on the other. He drew her slacks and panties down and away and kissed the hollows of her hips, making lazy, white-hot circles with the tip of his tongue.

Holly moaned with her need of him, so dazed she could barely see. When he shifted away from her and off the bed, she was stricken, until she realized that David was only removing his own clothing, that he would come back to her.

"Are you sure, Holly?" he asked softly as he stretched out beside her again, part of his lean, powerful body covering and making promises to hers.

"Yes," she managed to say.

He kissed her again, deeply and desperately, and their tongues engaged in a savage, fevered battle. His knee prodded her legs gently apart and then he was poised above her, bracing himself with his hands.

"God in heaven, Holly," he muttered hoarsely, "how I've wanted you...from the first..."

Holly's hands were moving up and down the sleek, rippled expanse of his back. She wanted to say something poetic, something memorable, but her arousal was such that she could no more than gasp his name.

David groaned and entered the sweet sanctum of her body, carefully and with a tenderness that deepened the love Holly already felt for him. He moved slowly at first, rhythmically, sheathing and unsheathing, reacquainting her with the long-forgotten feel of a man's possession.

Holly's few experiences with her fiancé long ago, had done nothing, nothing whatsoever, to prepare her for this. This was a glorious, blinding joy, one that centered all of her heart and all of her soul on the singular joining of this man's body with her own. She moved in time with him, making a soft, unselfconscious sound in her throat, a crooning, needing sound.

David's lips were everywhere, brushing her eyelids, tracing the line of her jaw, tasting her mouth. His tongue circled her lips in a way that was somehow territorial and fiercely arousing, and the pace he had set for her body increased by degrees until they both seemed to be hurling themselves at each other, frantic for a oneness that would consume them both.

When that moment came, David growled, his eyes closed, and shuddered upon Holly while she cried out and thrust her hips upward to enclose him as completely as she could.

They both sank into a sleeplike state for a time, their breathing ragged, eyes closed. David's fingers, tangled in Holly's hair, moved soothingly against her scalp. Then, suddenly and with devastating determination, he thrust himself free of her, cursing under his breath as he wrenched on his clothes.

Holly, shameless only moments before, now felt tawdry. She clasped the edge of the quilt covering her bed and pulled it over herself.

"David, what is it?" she finally dared to ask, watching wide-eyed as he completed the angry rite by jerking his boots back onto his feet.

He might have stormed out without saying anything at all if Holly hadn't spoken when she did, but then he froze, his back turned to her, rigid and impassive. "It was a mistake," he muttered at length.

"It was your idea!" Holly cried, wounded.

David lowered his head but did not turn around to face her. "Yes. It was my idea," he conceded raggedly.

"You feel guilty, don't you, David?"

Now he turned and met her eyes. "I'm sorry, Holly. I wanted you so badly I lost my head."

"You lost your head?" Holly was suddenly energized, electrified. But this time it was fury, not passion, that surged through her. Heedless of her nakedness, she flung back the quilt and bounded off the bed. "I beg your pardon?" she screamed.

David silenced her by laying three fingers gently, ever so gently, over her mouth. His eyes were dark with some pain that Holly couldn't understand and couldn't share. But whatever it was, she would gladly have traded her own confused, hurt feelings for it.

"Believe me when I tell you, Holly, that I've never wanted or needed a woman the way I needed you just now. Never. But it was a mistake. We can't let it happen again."

It would have hurt less, Holly was certain, if he'd slapped her. "What do you mean, it was a mistake? It was...it was..."

David kissed her forehead, wiped away the tears gathering at the corners of her eyes with practiced thumbs, then turned to walk away. He closed the door quietly behind him, but Holly waited until she was sure he was out of the house before flinging herself face down on the bed to cry.

## Chapter Six

The telephone rang. Sitting up on the bed, brushing her tangled hair back from her face, Holly reached out for the receiver, overriding the answering machine downstairs. Please, God, she prayed, let it be David.

"I left you two messages last night!" Craig blurted out the moment she said hello, "Don't you return your calls anymore, or is it something I said?"

Craig. Holly settled back on the pillows, which still bore the scent of David, and sighed. "I'm sorry, Craig. I was busy and—"

"You were *busy*? Good God, Holly! Remember me? I'm your brother, the man who is in trouble?"

Holly's throat was thick with despair, and her head ached. "We all have problems, Craig," she reminded him quietly, thinking of David Goddard.

"Sure, Holl. I know you're probably all torn up about whether to pay your Keogh Plan before the end of the year and what color to paint your toenails."

The sarcasm, following the scene with David as it did, was too much. "Listen, Craig. I care about you and you know it. I do everything I can to help you. But you're the one who got yourself into this mess; kindly remember that!"

He subsided. "I know. Holly, I'm so scared."

Tears smarted in Holly's eyes, sudden and hot. It was a surprise because she had been certain that there were none left to cry. Images of another Craig, bright and fit and funny, rose in her mind. Dear God, what had happened to change him this way? During the troubled years after their father's death, when their mother had been so confused and distracted, he had been Holly's strength, her lifeline.

"I know, Craig, I know. I beg of you, give yourself up."

"I can't, Holly. I just can't. You don't know how these guys treat a fink—"

"Craig, they're not going to hurt you. I'll have a lawyer present. You're still a citizen and you still have rights."

"Not anymore, I don't," he muttered. "I've had dealings with the KGB, Holly, and they know it."

"Why, Craig? Why did you turn to...to those people? Why did you do it?"

He made a strange sound and Holly was shattered to realize that he was crying. "I have a habit, Holly," he finally said.

Dread electrified Holly, and she bolted upright. "What kind of habit?" she whispered, her eyes wide and burning. "Dammit, Craig, *what kind of habit?*"

"Cocaine," he said.

"Oh, God," Holly groaned.

"Listen, I need money. Cindy managed to bring me what you sent, but that's gone now."

"No."

"What did you say?" Craig sniffled, and his voice sounded angry again.

"I said no, Craig. I'm not giving you money to buy poison! I absolutely will not!"

"Holly, I need—"

"You need help and I haven't been giving it to you! Oh, God, how could I have been so stupid—"

"Get the money, Holly. Send it to this address—" He rattled off a post office box number in a small Oregon town. "I mean it, Holly. If you don't, I'll be home for Christmas. And not to turn myself in."

"What are you saying?"

"I'm saying, Sister dear," he answered with tart patience, "that if you don't help me I'll take Toby on the road with me. That's what I'm saying."

"No! I won't let you! I won't let you expose him to that, drag him around the country—"

"You won't be able to stop me, Holly. I know where he goes to school, and I know where you live. And remember I'm a former federal agent—I'll find the kid no matter where you try to hide him."

"Craig!"

"Send the money," he said. He repeated the address once more and then hung up.

Slowly, her hand trembling so hard that she had to make several attempts before she could manage the task, Holly replaced the receiver in its cradle.

She sat there on the bed, cross-legged, her head in her hands, until she heard Toby downstairs. "Mom!"

he yelled exuberantly, probably still excited from his afternoon at the Ice Capades, "I'm home!"

Holly quickly leaped off the bed, found herself a robe and went down the stairs.

Toby was waiting at the bottom, his beloved face alight. "Geez, Mom," he said, barely able to stand still, "the ice show was great! They had the Flintstones and—" He stopped, taking in Holly's bathrobe and mussed hair with concern. "Are you sick, Mom?"

"No, darling, I'm not sick," Holly answered swiftly, forcing a smile to her face. "How did you get home, by the way? I thought I was supposed to pick you up."

"David brought me!" Toby sang, spreading his mittened hands for emphasis.

Holly swayed backward, just slightly, stunned. How could she have missed seeing David, when he was standing only a few feet away? Why hadn't she sensed that he was near?

"I hope you don't mind," David said quietly, but there was much, much more that his eyes were saying. They looked haunted, hollow.

Holly's temper flared, fanned by her fear, and she shifted her eyes to Toby's trusting, upturned face. "Don't you ever, ever get into anyone's car but mine, young man!" she hissed.

Toby retreated a step, looking as though she'd struck him. "But, Mom, David—"

David laid a quieting hand on the child's shoulder. "No, Tobe. She's right. We made a mistake, you and I."

Toby was not appeased. He darted one furious look at his trembling aunt and dashed off into another part of the house, probably to take solace in the late-afternoon cartoons he loved to watch on television.

"What are you doing here?" Holly half whispered, watching David, loving him even though her every instinct commanded her to tear out his hair.

"I couldn't stay away. Bringing Toby back from the ice show seemed the perfect excuse, so I did it. I'm sorry, Holly. I didn't mean to undermine your authority."

Holly held her chin high, but inwardly she was all too conscious of her appearance. "You are very, very good at finding excuses to keep tabs on me, aren't you, David?"

There was a thunderous silence, and David averted his eyes for a moment before meeting Holly's glare directly. "I love you, Holly."

Nothing he could have said would have surprised Holly more; she came a step nearer and her hand tightened on the banister until her knuckles ached. "What did you say?"

"Don't make me say it again, Holly. I already feel like enough of a fool as it is."

"Thanks a lot!"

"Just get dressed, will you? We need to talk, you and I. Not fight, not make love. Talk."

Holly stared at him for a few minutes and then, too confused to deal with anything, turned and dashed up the stairs. Safe in the shower stall, with hot water pouring down over her head and her newly awakened body, she rested her face against the tiled wall and tried to catch her breath.

David made himself at home in the kitchen, conscious of the glum little boy sitting slumped at the trestle table. "Your mom didn't mean to yell at you,

Tobe,'' he said, finding the coffee and the filters before pouring cold water into the top of the coffee maker.

''She's sure grouchy lately! And it's almost Christmas, too!''

David smiled somewhat sadly, and then turned to look directly at Toby, leaning back against the counter, the coffee maker chortling behind him. ''Sure enough, it is almost Christmas. Time to get a tree.''

Toby brightened a little, but he was still miffed. ''Yeah, I guess.'' His eyes strayed to Holly's desk, to the answering machine there, its light blinking frantically. ''She never listens to her calls, neither.''

For the first time since high school, David Goddard blushed. David Goddard, who had guarded presidents. ''She's been sort of busy.''

The child bounded off the bench, a study in impatience, and stomped over to the machine. Before David could intercede, he had pushed two buttons on the machine. There was a screeching sound as it rewound, and then it began to play. There were two brief messages from Holly's brother, followed by a long conversation that told David more than he really wanted to know.

Craig had a cocaine habit. He needed money. And he was in a town in Oregon, watching a certain post office box. When he began to talk about taking Toby from Holly, David strode across the room and turned off the machine abruptly.

Toby's eyes were brimming with tears, and his color, high from the cold weather outside and his time at the ice show, drained away. ''I want my mom!'' he blurted out, fleeing the room.

David swore and cast one despairing look at the ceiling before leaving the house. Five minutes later, from a phone booth outside a supermarket, he called the FBI.

Skyler, arriving unannounced, frowned at Holly. "My God," he muttered, "you look terrible!"

On this dismal Sunday morning, a soft snow was falling; a fire was crackling on the kitchen hearth. "Thanks, Sky," Holly said, stepping back to admit him to her kitchen. "A compliment always gives a day that little extra something."

"Don't be difficult," Skyler chided, taking off his stylish muffler and shaking it, a look of disapproval on his face. "I bring great tidings and all that."

Holly could have used some great tidings to offset the problems she was having with Craig and the confusion she felt over David's disappearance the day before. He'd seemed so eager to talk, but when she had finished her shower, dressed and gone downstairs, he had already left the house. After a quick search, she'd found Toby in his room, sobbing into his pillow, and the little boy had refused to tell her what was wrong.

Finally, he had fallen asleep. When he woke up later, Holly had offered him dinner, but he had refused. He was still silent this morning, and his mood added to Holly's growing collection of worries.

"So, what glad tidings do you bring?" she asked, going to the coffee maker and helping herself to her third cup since getting out of bed an hour earlier. After pouring a cup for Skyler, she sat down at the trestle table and nodded for him to do the same.

He took in her drawn face and the smudges under her eyes with puzzled concern. "Holly, what's wrong? You look—"

Holly held up one hand to stop him. "I know. Terrible."

"You're still in your bathrobe!" he marveled, shocked. Skyler didn't believe in looking less than one's best at any time of the day or night.

"Toby had bad dreams last night," she said, as though that were an explanation. She didn't add that she had been tormented by nightmares, too—when she had been able to sleep at all.

Skyler shrugged, looking helpless and a little annoyed. "What you need, what you both need, is a day in the country. Holly, let's drive out to my folks' farm and cut down a Christmas tree."

Holly knew that she shouldn't go, that she would be encouraging Skyler's affections if she went. Even though her involvement with David Goddard was an unholy mess, she didn't want to do that.

On the other hand, a drive in the wintry country-side would certainly be a pleasant distraction.

"Skyler, I—"

He sighed, and his fondness for Holly was naked in his eyes. "I know, Holly. You've been seeing someone else. Surely it isn't so serious that you can't spend a day with me?"

Holly's heart twisted slightly. The truth was, her entanglement with David was so serious that she *had* to spend a day with Skyler. If she stayed around the house, waiting for David or for another of Craig's devastating phone calls, she would surely go insane. And Toby needed the outing just as desperately as she did.

Gently, she reached across the table and closed her hand over Skyler's. She was surprised to find that he was trembling just a little. And she was saddened by what that probably meant. "I have been seeing David regularly, Sky. And I do care about him a great deal."

"I'd guessed that by the way you kept turning me down whenever I asked you out, Holly."

"I'm sorry," Holly replied softly, and she truly was. She had never wanted to hurt Skyler or anyone else, but she clearly had done just that.

"Say you'll come with me today, Holly. We'll find a couple of Christmas trees and Mom has a great dinner planned."

Skyler looked so hopeful that Holly wanted to cry. "Okay," she said. "Just give me a few minutes to get dressed and throw some breakfast together."

Skyler wasn't looking at her but into the depths of his coffee cup. "Don't bother with breakfast, Holly. We'll stop and eat on the way out of town."

Holly left the table, but she paused in the doorway of the kitchen, looking back at Skyler. Her throat ached and her answer came out sounding hoarse and raspy. "You're a good friend, Skyler Hollis. Do you know that?"

Skyler said nothing at all. After watching him for a silent, painful moment and wishing that things could be different, she hurried upstairs to get dressed.

"I'd like it better if David was taking us," Toby grumbled when Holly stopped by his room to ask him to get ready to go and find a Christmas tree.

So would I, Holly thought sadly, but she said, in a voice that quivered just the slightest bit, "Please don't be difficult, Toby. We need a dose of fresh air, you and I, and we're going to have it. Get ready, please. Skyler is treating us to breakfast.''

Glumly, Toby went about obeying. Just as glumly, Holly went on to the bathroom to take her shower.

The day with Skyler was, for Holly, a bittersweet experience. They were two people who knew that their relationship was going nowhere, and were trying to be cheerful despite it. All the same, it was a pleasant day, at least for Holly, giving her the time she needed to paste herself back together and think.

During breakfast she pondered Craig's cocaine problem and his threat to take Toby away. While she was frightened by the things her brother had said, she began to suspect that the part about stealing his son was just hysteria. Deluded though he was, Craig couldn't possibly believe that he would be capable, under the circumstances, of taking care of a child.

As for the cocaine, well, while it was certainly a horrible shock, it did explain a lot about Craig's treason. And that's what it was; Holly forced herself to accept the fact. It was treason.

After that, she was unable to finish her hearty breakfast, no matter how much a subdued Skyler might urge her. But what she had already eaten helped Holly considerably. She felt stronger, better able to cope.

Toby, too, was coming out of his curious mood, however reluctantly. He enjoyed eating in restaurants even when it involved spending time with Skyler.

When they left the restaurant, snow falling all around them and with an easy day ahead, Holly was able to put most of her problems out of her mind and chat with Skyler. Toby sat in the back seat, armed with a pocket trivia-game, shouting out an occasional question.

Skyler, in Holly's view, was uncommonly patient. "The Lone Ranger's uncle!" he called out once, in exuberant answer.

"Wrong," said Toby smugly, in the often-insensitive way of children. "It was Pinky Lee!"

Skyler rolled his eyes and tossed Holly a beleaguered look. She laughed because if she hadn't, she would have cried.

After an hour and a half of trivia, they reached the dairy farm owned by Skyler's parents. The Hollises were friendly people, and they greeted both Holly and Toby with comforting warmth. Hanging behind them, though, on the porch that stretched all the way around that carefully painted, solid old Victorian house, stood a young woman Holly had never seen before.

"Hello, Mary Ann," Skyler greeted the guest somewhat self-consciously. "How are you?"

A fetching blush rose in Mary Ann's pretty cheeks. "I'm all right. You?"

Skyler risked one broken glance at Holly and cleared his throat. "I'll get by," he answered gruffly.

Holly looked at Mary Ann again and hoped devoutly that Skyler would fall in love with her, here and now. It was obvious that the dark-haired, blue-eyed woman adored him—perhaps she and Skyler had grown up together and perhaps Mary Ann had always cared for him....

She brought herself up short. Fantasies. She was just weaving fantasies in hopes of making it easier to end her own relationship with Skyler.

"Mary Ann and I found some real good trees," Skyler's father announced cheerfully, and a glance at his leathery, good-natured face told Holly that he knew more about his son's relationship with the city lady than he was letting on.

Again Holly felt guilty. It was going to be so hard, telling Skyler she didn't want to see him anymore, even though he must certainly have guessed it from their conversation that morning.

After a round of coffee in the huge, high-ceilinged farmhouse kitchen—Toby, of course, had hot chocolate—everyone except Mrs. Hollis set out for the woods.

It was a bracingly cold day, and here in the country the snow was cleaner and, alas, deeper, making the jaunt to the woods rather hard going for Holly. Flinging back an occasional polite look, Mary Ann kept to the lead with Skyler and Toby.

Wearing high rubber boots and a heavy, plaid woolen coat that smelled pleasantly of tobacco smoke and hay, Mr. Hollis stayed beside the lagging Holly. Something in his manner inspired confidence, and Holly, feeling an innate need to talk with someone older and wiser, ventured, "Mary Ann and Skyler must have known each other for a long time."

Mr. Hollis smiled. "Since kindergarten," he replied, keeping his voice low, as Holly had, so that no one else would overhear. "I'm afraid it's pretty obvious that Mary Ann has her cap set for him. 'Bout broke her heart when he went away to the city to start that store of his. Mine and Mother's cracked a bit, too, as it happens."

Holly was saddened. Skyler was the Hollises' only son, though he did have one sister. Probably, his parents had hoped that he would want to take over the family farm someday. "I'm sorry," she said.

"Ain't your fault," came the quick reply, and a smile lighted the older man's eyes as Mary Ann picked up a handful of snow and flung it at Skyler, who shouted in good-natured protest and then returned the volley.

Toby, never one to stand on the sidelines, gathered up ammunition of his own and joined the battle.

"Mother was real pleased with that cookbook you sent up, the one with your autograph in it. She shows it to all her friends."

Holly didn't know what to say to that, beyond "thank you"; she wedged her hands into the pockets of her old coat and sighed, slogging grimly along in the wake of the escalating snow-war up ahead. Skyler, Mary Ann and Toby's laughter mingled, a bright song in the chilly, snow-flecked air.

"That's a fine boy you have there," Mr. Hollis persisted. Perhaps he sensed her need to talk and her paradoxical difficulty in doing so.

"Thank you. Toby is actually my brother's son, but I forget that most of the time, he seems like my own."

"Reckon if you take care of him and love him, then he is your own. It's the day-to-day of it that matters, you know."

"Yes," Holly agreed, thinking of Craig, remembering when he had been a fine father to Toby. But that had been several years ago, before Craig's wife, Allison, had died. Before his habit had driven him to sell out his own country.

"You don't say much, do you?"

Holly laughed. They were almost out of the pasture and into the stand of pine trees and Douglas firs that was their destination. "I'm usually more sociable," she said. "I'm sorry."

"No need to be sorry." He paused and caught her elbow in his strong, work-worn hand. His eyes were kind as they touched Holly's face. "A person's got to follow their heart, Miss Llewellyn. And sometimes it don't lead where they'd like it to, but they gotta go after it anyway."

So he did know that the relationship between her and Skyler was over. If it had ever really existed at all.

"I'm hoping that Skyler will find someone else soon," she said, her voice trembling a little. Cool snowflakes collected on her eyelashes and chilled her cheeks, and Holly glanced ahead at the laughing Mary Ann. "Maybe..."

Mr. Hollis looked pleased, and he gave a guffaw of laughter. "Maybe so," he agreed.

As if to lend the theory credence, Skyler lunged at a gleefully shrieking Mary Ann and threw her down into the snow, rubbing a handful in her face. She came up sputtering and laughing, making exuberant threats. Toby, having watched all this with mingled delight and uncertainty, hurled a questioning look back at Holly.

It's all right, she told him with her smile, and his face was again alight with the joys of the day.

There was a bewildering array of trees to choose from, but Holly, her jeans snow-sodden to her knees, was not inclined to be persnickety. Skyler shook out a fragrant fir that stood about seven feet tall and appeared to be symmetrical, and she nodded in answer to the question in his eyes.

Mr. Hollis handed over the small hatchet he carried, saying he was "too derned old" for such carryings-on, and Skyler chopped down the tree.

With Toby frolicking at his heels like a puppy—for this was proof that Christmas, that most elusive of childhood days, was truly coming—Skyler began dragging the tree back toward the house.

"Don't you want a tree for yourself?" Holly asked him, ignoring the territorial looks from Mary Ann. These, she supposed, were her just due for falling into step beside Skyler.

"I'll get one another time," he said softly.

Holly knew then that the had contrived the whole idea of tracking down a Christmas tree for her benefit; after all, it was still three full weeks until the holiday. He had seen how upset she was, sensed that she was frazzled and overwrought, and tried to help.

A feeling like love but sadly different twisted in her throat. "Thank you, Sky," she said gently.

Skyler only shrugged, but when he shifted his attention to Mary Ann and started teasing her about gaining weight since he'd seen her last—she was trim enough to be a fashion model—his voice was a determinedly cheerful boom.

Mary Ann gloried in the attention, though she pretended to be outraged, and Toby jumped and leaped in the scratchy snow trail left in the wake of the fallen tree, his cheeks pink, his china-blue eyes shining. How mercifully innocent he was just now, Holly thought, how unaware he still was of the complications that lay ahead in the process of growing up.

They ate a sumptuous dinner of fried chicken, mashed potatoes and country gravy, biscuits, and green beans that Mrs. Hollis had put up herself. She and Mary Ann talked so easily about farm things; the prices they could get for cream and eggs, the patterns they would use for sewing their Christmas dresses, whether to plant peas on St. Valentine's Day or later on, in March.

Holly listened with interest and a sort of weary nostalgia, and when the meal was over, she volunteered to do the dishes. Mrs. Hollis, having worked in the kitchen all day, was obviously tired.

Skyler and Mr. Hollis and Toby went outside to tie the Christmas tree to the roof of Skyler's car, and Mrs. Hollis retired to the living room to "put her feet up for a spell." Mary Ann, her eyes looking everywhere but at Holly, stayed to help with the dishes.

Holly felt a need to put Skyler's friend at ease. After all, Mary Ann belonged here, fitting in better than Holly herself ever could.

"You and Sky have been friends for a long time," she said quietly, taking up a flour-sack dish towel when Mary Ann had elbowed her away from the sink.

Now Mary Ann's dark, beautiful eyes swung to Holly's face, confused, but wary and full of challenge. "I love Skyler," she said in a low, earnest voice.

Holly smiled. "I know," she answered. "Toby and I won't be back here anymore after today."

There was a silence while Mary Ann absorbed that statement and dealt with it in her own way. Finally, she turned a bright smile on Holly. "It was good to meet you all the same," she said.

Holly laughed, and after that, the two women worked in swift accord, putting the kitchen right again in no time at all.

## Chapter Seven

Toby's eyes were round and sleepy as he looked up at Holly, and he yawned. "Let's decorate the Christmas tree," he suggested, valiant in the face of his fatigue.

Holly laughed and rumpled his hair. "Tomorrow, sweetheart. After school."

With an acquiescent shrug, he turned and scampered up the stairs, stopping midway to look at Skyler and say, "Thanks for taking us to the country. It was real neat."

Skyler shoved his hands into the pockets of his jacket, looking ill at ease and shy. He didn't truly belong in this house any longer, and that saddened Holly even though she knew it was for the best. "You're welcome, kid," he said.

Holly suppressed a tired smile. Some things didn't change. "Will you stay for coffee, Skyler?" she asked.

He shook his immaculately groomed head. "I don't think that would be a good idea." Toby was gone by then, busy getting ready for bed. "It's over, isn't it, Holly?" he added in a sad voice.

"Yes," she said quietly. "I'm sorry."

There was a painful silence, and then Skyler sighed and shrugged his shoulders. When he met Holly's eyes again, he was smiling with an obvious effort. "I'd better bring in the tree before I go. Where do you want it, Holly?"

Holly gestured vaguely toward the living room, and Skyler cleared his throat as though he might say something more. Then he ran one hand through his neatly styled hair, something Holly had never seen him do, and turned away without speaking at all.

The tree stood in the corner of the dimly lit living room, leaning, lushly green and fragrant, into the corner. There were no decorations on its boughs just yet, and to Holly, all alone now that Toby was asleep and Skyler had gone home, it was a forlorn sight.

She sighed, knowing that for all the exercise and fresh air of the day just ending, sleep would elude her. She turned off the living-room lights and went into the kitchen, where she poured a cup of coffee and sat down at the trestle table.

"Coffee," she mocked herself, lifting the cup. "Just what your average insomniac needs before bed."

It was then that the flashing light on the answering machine caught Holly's eye. Resigned—one couldn't shut out the world forever—she stood up and crossed the room to her desk, pressing the rewind button and then the one marked Play.

The first voice on the recording was Elaine's, saying that she had the flu and might not make it to work the next day. The second belonged to Holly's housekeeper, promising to come in to clean on Tuesday.

Holly frowned. This was strange. What had happened to those two brief messages from Craig? He'd said he'd called twice.

A third voice came on, jolting her out of her reflections. David's voice.

"Holly, call me, will you please? My number is 555-6782. It's important, so don't worry about the time."

Holly stood frozen in that lonely kitchen, such a busy place in the daytime but so echoingly empty now. Why should she call David after the way he'd treated her? Hadn't he made love to her and then said they'd made a mistake and left her alone with her confusion and her conscience? And then he'd come back, saying that he loved her, saying that they needed to talk— and disappeared before they could!

She let the answering machine run on until she was certain there were no more messages. Something besides the two vanished calls from Craig niggled at the back of her mind but she couldn't quite grasp what it was.

David answered on the first ring, not with a hello but with his name. And that bothered Holly, too.

To cover her uneasiness, she blurted out, "David, if this is a game, I don't want to play! You said we needed to talk before, and then you just left!"

His sigh came, a raspy sound, over the wire that linked them together so tenuously. "Something came up, Holly, and I had to leave. I'm sorry."

Holly sank into her desk chair, turning the telephone cord in the fingers of one hand. "Toby was very upset, David. Do you know why?"

David hesitated and finally said, "No."

He was lying. Holly knew he was lying. But why? Whatever doubts she might have about David Goddard, she was absolutely certain that he would never do or say anything to put Toby in such a state. "You said you wanted to talk," she prompted coldly.

"I do. But not over a wire. Holly, could I come over? Please?"

Holly sighed and glanced ruefully at the Seth Thomas clock on the kitchen mantelpiece. "It's late, David—after eleven."

"Do you think you'll sleep tonight if we don't talk?" he asked.

Holly felt her face flushing. "That's all we're going to do—provided I agree to your visit, that is. Toby's home and—"

"I didn't ask you to go to bed with me, Holly," came the patient reply. "I really do want to talk with you. In person."

Holly's face grew hotter still, and she closed her eyes as memories of David's lovemaking washed over her in a heated, crushing wave. Perhaps that was what gave her the courage to refuse—if it was courage. "We can talk tomorrow, David. I've had a long day, and I'm tired."

"Holly—"

"Tomorrow," she said firmly.

"Tomorrow," he sighed, and then the line went dead. Holly hung up the telephone, frowned at the answering machine for just a moment and then went upstairs to bed.

Surprisingly, she slept soundly that night, without the dreams that had been troubling her so much.

Getting Toby off to school in the morning was a madness of lost textbooks and half-eaten oatmeal, as usual. Elaine called to say that she was still sick and definitely wouldn't be over.

Once she was alone, Holly eyed the work waiting on her desk with trepidation. Her newspaper column was due in two days and needed to be extensively rewritten, but she couldn't work up the self-discipline necessary to do the job.

It was almost a relief when David knocked at the glass panes in the kitchen door and then let himself in at Holly's somber nod. By that time, she had lugged the huge boxes of Christmas-tree decorations down from the attic and was going through the newspaper-wrapped contents in search of the red and green stand.

"I'm sorry about last Saturday, Holly," he said quietly.

Holly's face heated again, and then chilled. There was a guilty, reluctant look about David, as though he had something important to say, something that he dreaded saying.

"That's okay," Holly lied, turning her attention back to the ornaments and the pieces of the large creche left her by her grandmother. "Have some coffee."

"Where were you yesterday?" David asked, finding the cups and rattling the coffee maker's glass decanter against the mug when he tried to fill it.

It gave Holly a perverse sort of pleasure to answer, "Skyler took Toby and me up to his parents' farm to look for a Christmas tree."

David was silent for so long that Holly finally had to turn around and look at him. Still wearing his brown leather jacket, he was watching her with unreadable indigo eyes, leaning back against the counter as he sipped the too hot coffee.

"Are you in love with him, Holly?"

Holly sighed, unwrapping one of the three wise men and turning the large porcelain figure in her hands. "No. In fact, I told Skyler last night that we shouldn't see each other anymore."

There was another silence, broken at long last by David's noncommital, "I see."

And suddenly Holly was furious. She whirled, the wise man still in her hands, and cried, "Dammit, David, you said you wanted to talk! It was your idea, remember?"

A half smile curved his lips. "Isn't that what we're doing? Talking?"

"No, damn you, it isn't! We're...we're shadow-boxing!"

David sighed, set his steaming mug of coffee aside and shrugged out of his jacket, laying it over the back of a kitchen chair without particular concern. Holly had a feeling that he was used to expensive things, which the jacket obviously was.

"You're right," he said. "We are sparring. Holly, I meant it when I told you that I love you."

Holly's hands were trembling; she set down the endangered wise man. "So you did," she finally croaked out, keeping her head averted because there were sudden, inexplicable tears in her eyes and she couldn't bear for him to see them. "But something is terribly wrong between us, David. I know it; I sense it. You're keeping something from me."

He came to her then and clasped her shoulders in his hands. His throat worked fruitlessly for a moment, as though it were difficult for him to speak. "Whatever happens, Holly, remember that I love you. When we made love the other day—"

Holly pulled away from him, both drawn to him and frightened. "When we made love, you said it was a mistake," she reminded him, wounded by the memory.

The Christmas-tree stand was uncovered, and she pulled it out of the box. David took it from her hands and put it aside.

"Look at me, Holly."

Holly didn't want to obey, but she did. She had to.

"I thought I loved Marleen," he said slowly, his hands on Holly's shoulders again, firm and strong. "When she left, I hurt for a long, long time. And then it got so that I didn't feel anything, didn't want to feel anything. I had a lot of affairs, Holly—I'm not denying that—but until I met you I didn't think it was possible for me to really care about another woman."

One tear sneaked down Holly's face and she brought one hand up betwen David's arms to wipe it away. "Still something is wrong...I..."

He bent and kissed her briefly, tenderly. "Just trust me, Holly. I know that's a lot to ask, but I'm asking you."

"Something awful is going to happen!" Holly cried, frantic.

"Maybe. Sometimes things happen that are very painful at the time, but they're still for the best. And I'll be on the other side, waiting for you."

He was being so damned cryptic! Holly wanted to pound his chest with her fists, to claw out his eyes.

Unfortunately, another part of her wanted to take David by the hand and lead him upstairs to that bed where they had made such sweet love, where she had been transformed, if only temporarily, into a woman with no problems, no doubts, no pain.

David caught her chin in his hand and lifted her face so that she had to look directly into his eyes. "I love you," he repeated slowly. "Whatever happens, I don't want you to forget that, Holly. Promise me that much."

She swallowed hard. "Tell me what you know, David. Who you are. What do you want—"

"I want you."

"You are being deliberately obtuse!"

He smiled, but it was a sad smile, and something vital lay broken in his eyes. He released Holly and took up the Christmas-tree stand, turning it slowly in his hands. "I'll set the tree up for you, if you want."

Holly bit her lower lip and then nodded. It was obvious that she wasn't going to get any more information out of David, but God help her, she didn't want him to go. Not yet.

"Thank you," she managed to say.

Setting the tree in its stand proved to be just what David and Holly needed to lighten the impossible weight of the situation. By the time Holly was finally willing to admit that the tree was as straight as it could possibly be, they were both laughing.

While David was washing the pitch from his hands, Holly impulsively lighted a fire in the living-room hearth and put on a tape of instrumental Christmas music. As if to accommodate her oddly festive mood, a soft snow began to drift past the windows.

I'm crazy, Holly thought. I'm definitely certifiable. Half an hour ago, I was crying and now, just because David and I put up the Christmas tree, I'm lighting fires and playing music and setting the stage for something that shouldn't happen.

David returned, a cautious smile on his face. Without saying a word, he caught Holly's hand in his, sat down on the couch and pulled her gently into his lap. He smelled deliciously of fresh air and pine, and his blue eyes, often so disturbing, were as warm as the snapping fire on the hearth.

"I love you, David," Holly blurted out without stopping to think. How could she think when he was holding her that way, his hands making tender circles on her shoulder blades?

He laughed. "At last you admit it."

Holly was honestly surprised that she hadn't said the words before. God knew, the truth of them had been as much a part of her as her breath and her heartbeat, almost from the first. "David—"

He turned her on his lap and kissed her. "Shh. It's Christmas."

Holly was gasping by the time the kiss ended. She knew that her hair was probably mussed and her cheeks flushed. "It is *not* Christmas—"

David's face was buried in her neck, his lips making tantalizing forays along its pulsing length. "Woman," he groaned, and the word was at once a reprimand and the most flagrant praise. "You argue about everything."

The buttons on Holly's blouse were opening, one by one, and his mouth was following the ever-deepening vee of bared flesh intrepidly. Heat so intense that it bordered on pain surged through Holly as he explored the rounded side of one breast and nuzzled that side of her bra down far enough to bare what he sought.

"Ooooh," she groaned as he took brazen nips at the aching nipple and then suckled it. And all her doubts fled before the flames of her passion and his.

As David undressed her, never really ceasing his tender assault on her throbbing senses, all memory fled. By the time he had subjected her to the scandalously delicious release meant to prepare her for final conquering, Holly couldn't have recited her own name.

He did not enter her gently this time, but with a thrust that was fiercely pleasurable for Holly. Her hands moved wildly over the muscle-ridged expanse of his bare back, pleading, urging.

There was something sweetly wicked about making love on the living-room couch, and Holly's passion was heightened by it, as, she sensed, was David's.

When the moment of scalding release came, it enfolded them both. David was kissing Holly as they moved together, and his moans of tender defeat echoed inside her mouth, mingling with her own fevered cries.

They lay entwined for some time afterward, their breathing ragged, their hearts pounding as though to break past flesh and bone and be bonded together.

This time, to Holly's enormous relief, there was no talk about their lovemaking being a mistake. And this time David did not leave her.

No, they showered together, laughing and flinging soapsuds at each other at first, later slipping into passion again. They made love a second time, their bodies still slick with water, on Holly's bed. After that, they dressed and made a tongue-in-cheek agreement to behave themselves.

When Toby got home from school, he found them in the living room, sorting the lights that would set the freshly cut Christmas tree aglow. His greeting to David was a whoop of delight and a hurling of his small, solid body into the man's arms. David laughed and pretended to be falling under the weight, and Holly, watching them both, was more certain of her love for this enigmatic man than ever before.

They worked, the three of them, until dinner time, transforming the fragrant tree into a thing of glory. By the time the last glass ball was hung and the last strand of tinsel had been draped from just the right bough, it was dark outside.

"You can fix dinner now, Mom!" Toby announced magnanimously, his eyes on the shimmering wonder of the Christmas tree. "Us men are starved."

David laughed and shook his head. "Us men," he corrected Toby with mock sternness, "are going for take-out chicken. Your mom has done enough for one day."

Holly's eyes linked with David's and she blushed. That "enough" didn't bear recounting. "You don't have to go out. We've got lots of food in the freezer."

"Yuk," Toby complained. "I'm tired of egg rolls. I want to go with David to get chicken."

Both of her men stood watching her, waiting for her approval. "Okay," she relented, smiling even though she tried to look insulted. "But you stay with David, Toby Llewellyn. Don't go wandering off and don't ask for two deserts. Or for pop."

Toby flung David a beleaguered look. "I'm not allowed to eat much sugar," he complained.

David chuckled and rumpled Toby's corn-silk hair. "You're so abused. Tell me your sad story in the car, will you?"

And after David had kissed Holly soundly but briefly, they were off.

Holly sat alone in the living room with the lamps turned off, admiring the lights of the Christmas tree. "When it comes to glow, Tree," she said aloud, "you've got nothing on me."

David liked being with Toby, and he had certainly enjoyed the day. Still, Craig Llewellyn was much in his thoughts as he navigated the snow-slicked roads in the Camaro he had rented after returning the brown sedan.

The little boy, fastened firmly into the seat belt on the passenger side, chattered on and on about the Christmas tree, the day they'd flown model airplanes in the park and the trip to Skyler Hollis's family's farm. David listened patiently, though in actuality he was going over the facts Walt Zigman had given him during their last telephone conversation.

Craig Llewellyn had managed to elude the FBI in that little Oregon town, just as he had in L.A. He was smart, Llewellyn was, and slippery. But he wasn't smart enough.

David knew that he would appear in Spokane very soon. And he was worried about Llewellyn's threat, overheard the day Toby had impulsively turned on Holly's answering machine and replayed her conversation with her brother. She obviously didn't know that David had heard the recording; maybe she didn't even realize that the machine had been on when she'd picked up the telephone.

He glanced at Craig's son and wondered how cocaine could have been bigger than such a treasure of a child. God, if this boy were his own...

David stopped himself. Once this thing with Craig actually broke, there would probably be little left of what he and Holly shared. She would hate him and so would the boy. It was a grim irony that he'd chosen her of all people, to fall in love with.

David seemed subdued when he and Toby returned with the take-out chicken. His eyes dodged Holly's and his contributions to the conversation were few and far between.

"What's wrong?" she asked, when a grumbling Toby had been settled at the trestle table to do his homework, and they were alone again beside the Christmas tree.

"I guess I'm tired," he said.

Holly was on the verge of tears. Was he going to spoil the day, after all they'd shared? Was he going to start talking "mistake" again?

"I guess you're shutting me out," Holly argued evenly. "And I don't understand it, David. Not after today. You can't make love to me and then treat me as though I'm some bad habit you wish you could break."

The word "habit" hung between them, or so it seemed to Holly. But David couldn't know about Craig's confessions to her concerning cocaine; there was no way he could know that.

"I can't do this problem!" Toby wailed from the kitchen. "Somebody help me!"

"I'll do it," David volunteered, his eyes still averted. And a moment later, he was turning his back on Holly and striding off toward the kitchen. He remained there until Toby's homework was done and it was bedtime.

While Holly appreciated the help David gave Toby—math was her secret nemesis—she felt a bit put out, too. How had things changed so completely, just in the time it took David to go and buy the take-out chicken?

When she came downstairs, having tucked Toby into bed and heard his prayers, David was sitting in front of the living-room fire, staring ponderously into the flames as though some drama were being played out there.

Holly needed a moment to think, to collect herself; where this man was concerned, she had a way of plunging over emotional precipices, of saying and doing all the wrong things. Turning into the kitchen, she suddenly halted, stunned.

Craig was standing there, leaning casually against the counter, a cup of hot coffee in his hand. He looked so ragged and thin, with a fevered light in his eyes that made Holly despair.

"Craig," she whispered.

He toasted her sardonically with a lift of his coffee cup. "You didn't send the money," he said.

Holly could barely breathe, so great was her shock at seeing this wasted parody of the man who had been her brother. His filthy army fatigue jacket seemed two sizes too large and his eyes were sunken and haunted. "Craig, I couldn't," she said, keeping her voice low for fear that David would hear. "I didn't have a chance. You only called on Saturday..."

Craig's eyes swept the room, as though he might be assessing the value of things he saw there. "That guy helping Toby with his homework. Who is he?"

"Keep your voice down! He's still here!"

Craig's thin shoulders lifted in an impertinent shrug. "What's his name and where did you meet him?"

Holly sighed, half-sick with surprise and confusion, afraid that David would hear Craig and, conversely, afraid that he wouldn't. "His name is David Goddard and I met him in a class I'm teaching."

"I thought so. I remember him from the good old days."

"You—you what?"

"I remember him. He's a Secret Service agent, Holly. Or didn't he tell you that? I'll bet he asks a lot of questions about your misguided big brother, doesn't he?"

The room swayed around Holly, rising and falling, tilting at stomach-clenching angles.

"You mean you didn't even suspect?" Craig taunted in leisurely tones. "He must be pretty good."

Holly had suspected; she *had*. So why was it such a brutal surprise? She groped for the trestle table's sturdy edge, collapsing onto the bench. "Oh, my God. My God."

"The Secret Service doesn't usually handle this sort of thing," Craig speculated idly. "Must be connected to our dear cousin Howard, the never and future king."

It happened then; David came through the doorway. Holly heard him, felt him there, but could not look at him. Or at Craig.

"Llewellyn," he said, and Holly supposed it was an offhand greeting, though David had given the name no tone at all.

"Goddard," Craig replied calmly.

Holly looked up then, afraid. Suppose Craig had a gun? Suppose— "Would you leave us alone, please?" Craig asked her companionably. "We're old friends."

Holly hadn't the strength to rise from that bench at the trestle table, and even if she had, she still would have stayed.

She darted a look from one expressionless man to the other, praying that there would be no violence, praying that Toby wouldn't stumble in.

David didn't so much as glance in her direction, and when he spoke again, he addressed Craig. "This can be easy, Llewellyn, or it can be difficult. The choice is yours."

Craig laughed and then horrified his stunned sister by pulling a pistol from beneath his tattered army coat and laying it on the table. "I'll take it easy," he said. "Besides, the bushes outside are probably crawling with crew cuts by now. I'm not so far gone that I don't know you guys have been watching this place."

David took up the pistol deftly and unloaded the chamber, slipping the bullets into his pocket. His gaze slid to Holly just for a moment, and there was nothing in it to indicate that they had ever laughed together, ever been lovers.

When he went to the door to admit the inevitable agents, Holly sagged against the table's edge and covered her face with both hands.

## Chapter Eight

By morning, the news of Craig Llewellyn's "dramatic" capture was all over the newspapers. It was on television; it was on the radio. And it was in Elaine's face when she returned to work, largely recovered from her flu and wide-eyed with concern.

Holly sat blindly at the trestle table, a newspaper spread out before her.

Elaine took off her coat and sat down on the bench across from Holly. Being a true friend, she didn't ask why she had never heard anything about Craig before. "Are you going to let Toby go to school today?"

Holly sighed. "I don't know. Oh, Elaine, I don't know anything."

"It must have been awful."

Images of FBI agents surging into her kitchen throbbed in Holly's mind. Images of David, so cold, so quiet, so determined. "At least Toby slept through it all," she managed to say.

Elaine's hand came across the table to squeeze Holly's. "David Goddard—"

"Don't mention that man's name in this house, Elaine! Not ever again!" Holly flared, her eyes filling with tears of betrayal and fury.

"You were in love with him," Elaine said flatly. "I thought so."

"He wasn't in love with me!" Holly wailed. "Oh, Elaine, it was all an act from the first! I should have known—I *did* know but I wouldn't listen to my own instincts."

"That's very hard to do sometimes," Elaine comforted quietly. "Did David tell you that he cared for you?"

"Yes! But he lied—he only wanted to find Craig!"

"Maybe he didn't lie, Holly. Maybe he meant what he said."

"He lied. He wanted my brother." Holly was calmer now, though her heart was still thick with despair and raw sobs lurked beneath her carefully modulated words. "He lied."

"Well," Elaine said, "one thing is for certain: we're not going to get any work done today. And I don't think Toby should go to school until things quiet down a bit, do you?"

Holly shook her head. Eventually, the little boy was going to have to face the things his father had done, but she wanted him to hear the truth directly from her, and not on the school grounds. "C-could you take him home with you, just for the day? I'm afraid there will be reporters..."

"You know I'll do anything I can to help. What about your class tonight, Holly? Are you going to go ahead with that, or shall I call everyone and tell them the course has been canceled?"

Again Holly shook her head. "I'll go crazy if I don't keep on working."

"What if David comes to class?" Elaine asked softly.

"I don't think even he would have that kind of gall. But if he does show up, I have a few things I want to say to him, you can bet on that!"

"It might be better to listen to what he has to say, Holly. I can't believe he—"

"Believe it. I was just something above and beyond the call of duty to him, Elaine. A means to an end."

Elaine looked as though she might want to say more, but she held her tongue. The telephone began to ring and she leaped up to answer it, her voice crisp and in charge.

"Do you want to talk to the press, Holly?" she asked after a few words with the caller, her hand over the mouthpiece.

"No!" Holly cried.

"I'm sorry," Elaine said into the receiver, "Ms. Llewellyn has no comment." With that, she hung up and turned on the answering machine to record a similar message for any future callers, setting it to pick up automatically.

And it was then, of all times, that Holly remembered what it was that had eluded her before, concerning the answering machine. After leaving those two vanished messages, Craig had called her again and the machine had been on. It would have recorded both sides of the conversation between her and her brother.

David Goddard had listened to that conversation, and he had erased it from the machine! He would have heard Craig mention the town in Oregon, the cocaine habit. And when the FBI had failed to find her brother there, he had no doubt deduced that Craig was desperate enough to come to Holly.

Which explained, of course, why he had spent the day there. Putting up the Christmas tree. Making love to Holly, going out for fast food so she wouldn't have to cook. And, finally, helping Toby with his homework. All very neat and professional.

In that moment of realization, if David had been standing before her, Holly was certain she could have killed him without hesitation.

Elaine had gone upstairs to fetch Toby, and the back door burst open and snapped closed again so forcibly that Holly was startled out of her grisly reflections.

Madge Elkins, the housekeeper, was turning the lock and getting out of her coat at the same time. "Good Lord, there must be a hundred reporters and TV people out there, Holly. They chased me up the driveway!"

Like an automaton, Holly got up from the bench and went to the window over the sink. Sure enough, the backyard was full of paparazzi. So, probably, was the sidewalk out front.

If they step on my tulips, Holly thought ferociously, stomping through the house. And there they were, dozens of them, with cameras of every sort in their hands and avid looks on their faces.

Holly flung open a window in the living room and yelled, "Get out of my flower beds!" Before so much as one question could be asked, she slammed the window shut again, so that their sudden burst of words only bounced off the glass, a dull, babbling sound.

In the kitchen, Elaine and Toby were getting ready to make a break for it. Holly knelt in front of her nephew and held his small shoulders in her hands, hurting for the confusion and fear in his face.

"Tobe, everything is going to be okay," she said in a voice that didn't sound the least bit like her own. "It really is."

"Why are all those people out there? What did we do?"

"We didn't do anything. Toby, your dad was arrested last night and they want to ask us about him. You don't have to say anything at all to them; just stay close to Elaine."

Toby's eyes were wide and frightened. "Dad was arrested? Why?"

There was no choice but to be honest. Now, at this late date, Holly wished she had told Toby about Craig to prepare him for this envitable disaster. "Your dad has a lot of problems, Tobe. Remember that day in the park, when I told you that he does bad things sometimes?"

"They put bad people in jail!" Toby protested, his lower lip jutting out.

"The police are not our enemies, Toby. It might not seem so right now, but being arrested was the best thing that could have happened to your dad. Now he'll get the help he needs."

Toby was clearly still confused, but he was calmer. Madge, on the other hand, was fidgety, standing at the kitchen window and peering out.

"I don't know if you should try to get past them, Elaine," she fretted. "It might be better to stay here."

This particular dilemma had been gnawing at Holly, too. She kissed Toby's forehead and stood up again, wondering what to do. It was then that David appeared at the back door, his breath a white fog in the winter air, his face set and determined. Holly would certainly not have admitted him, but Elaine did just that, before she could protest.

He barely glanced in Holly's direction, speaking instead to Elaine as he distractedly ruffled Toby's hair and then drew the child against him. Not knowing of David's part in this debacle, the little boy held on to the man as if for dear life. "What's the plan?"

Holly simmered, too furious to speak, but Elaine answered David's question as though he had every right to be there, every right to ask such a thing.

"I want to take Toby over to my place, but we're not sure about shuffling him through that crowd."

David, still not sparing so much as a look for Holly, nodded crisply and reached down with one arm, lifting Toby to ride on his hip. He smiled, actually smiled, into the child's trusting face. "Tell you what, slugger. I'll take you to Elaine's car. You just pretend those people aren't even there, okay?"

"Do they want to hurt me?" Toby asked in a tone that twisted Holly's heart.

"No way," David said confidently. "They want to ask you questions, just like your teachers do at school. But we don't have time to talk, do we?"

"No," grinned Toby, wrapping his arms around David's neck. "We don't want to talk."

David's eyes shifted to Holly's then, meeting her gaze squarely. And the expression in those fathomless indigo depths said that he was not apologizing for Craig's capture.

Holly would not have expected him to do that. Craig was a sick man and his arrest, as she had told Toby in other words, was, though painful, the end of a long nightmare. No, it was the way David had used her that hurt. The way he had insinuated himself into her life, caused her to care for him and lied again and again, both by word and by action, about his own feelings.

Now, though he hadn't said a word, he was asking her permission before plunging into the crowd of TV and newspaper people. Seeing the trust in Toby's face, knowing it would be better if he spent the day away from the house, she was forced to give that permission. She nodded, letting her eyes tell David Goddard that despite this concession, the distance between them could never be bridged.

With Elaine at his heels and Toby perched on his hip, David opened the kitchen door and went out. Madge fretted and fussed at the window; she was braver than Holly, who could not bear to look.

"They made it!" the housekeeper crowed after a few seconds of terrible suspense.

"D-David isn't on his way back in here, is he?" Holly ventured to ask, wringing her hands.

"No," Madge replied, apparently innocent of the intrigue that had just taken place between her employer and the man in question. "His car must be out front, because he went the other way. Maybe he's going to follow Elaine and Toby to make sure they aren't bothered en route."

The possibility that some of the reporters might trail after Elaine had not occurred to Holly until then, and she was jarred by it. "You don't suppose they will, do you? You don't suppose these...these people will bother Elaine and Toby?''

"They'll stay here," Madge said confidently, her face still pressed to the window. One of her hands waved in an annoyed gesture. "Get out of there!" she shouted to someone outside. "You'll crush the lilac bush! You! Yes, you! Leave that birdbath alone!"

Despite everything, Holly had to laugh at the ludicrous comedy of it all. She poured herself a cup of coffee and went to her desk in the corner of the room, as though this were any ordinary day. The way the answering machine kept picking up on phone calls proved, of course, that it wasn't, as did the horde Madge had ordered away from the birdbath and the lilac bushes. Until Elaine called to say that they had arrived at Roy's mother's house out in the Spokane Valley, she left the machine's volume up so that she could hear each caller.

Grasping the receiver quickly, she spoke with Elaine and, for a few moments, with a gleefully excited Toby. It seemed that the whole matter had become an adventure to him, which was a relief to his aunt. After glorying in the fact that he didn't have to go to school that day, he hung up, and Holly pushed the volume button on the machine to its lowest setting before starting to work on her column.

Toward midmorning the media people got tired of standing around in the cold weather and began to straggle away, a few at a time, until the yard and driveway were empty again.

One would almost have thought that nothing abnormal had happened at all, Holly reflected as she worked on her cooking column and Madge dusted and vacuumed in another part of the house.

The answering machine was a reminder, of course; the moment one message had been left, another caller would try to get through.

But when Holly finished her column, which was surprisingly good, she thought, under the circumstances, she began to think about David again, and how he had betrayed her. How he had seduced her.

She didn't quite dare to go outside, but if she didn't work off some of her anger, and soon, she knew she was going to be tearing her hair. Staunchly, Holly went upstairs and exchanged her jeans and sweater for a pink jogging-suit with stripes of white running the length of each arm and each leg. She pinned up her hair, drew a deep breath and made her way to the family room just off the kitchen, where the mini-trampoline was kept.

Rolling it out of a closet, she set it on its sturdy legs. She switched on the TV to a cable channel devoted exclusively to old movies and bounced furiously on the trampoline while watching Claudette Colbert win Fred MacMurray's heart.

Holly ran, she did jumping-jacks and then she just bounced again. Up and down, higher and higher she went, but she couldn't escape the fact that she loved David Goddard, no matter how hard she tried to distract herself.

The housekeeper, like Elaine, seemed kindly disposed toward David. Or, at least, she let him into the house when he knocked tentatively at the kitchen door.

"Where is she?" he asked.

The woman went back to the table, where she had been eating lunch and following the details of Craig

Llewellyn's arrest on the black-and-white screen of a TV roughly the size of a postcard. "In there," she gestured toward the inner doorway, "trying to bounce herself through the family-room ceiling."

David frowned and wedged his hands nervously into his pockets before going to the doorway to investigate. Holly was wearing a pink sweat suit, her soft blond hair pinned up haphazardly, her breathing audible even over the television set she was watching.

Her back was turned to David and she didn't hear his approach, for she kept right on bouncing. Bouncing. A shimmering film of perspiration shone from beneath the loose tendrils of honey-colored hair at the nape of her neck. "Don't you trust him, Claudette," she sputtered out. "All men are rat finks."

David felt a lot of things at that moment: sympathy, regret and, most of all, a desire to wrench Holly Llewellyn off that damned jogger-thing and make love to her on the family-room floor.

He rounded Holly and stood before her, inwardly bracing himself for what he knew was coming.

Her beautiful aquamarine eyes, somewhat swollen and red, widened at the sight of him. He felt like Benedict Arnold crashing a party at George and Martha's place. At least she'd stopped that damned bouncing.

"Get the hell out of my house!" she hissed, her perfect cheekbones flaring to the color of her sweat suit, her hands clenched into fists at her sides.

"No. I'm not going anywhere until you get down off that thing and talk to me."

"I'll call the police!"

"I don't think so. Besides, I probably have more sway with them than you do." He turned, admired Claudette Colbert's unique face for one steadying moment and then switched off the TV. "Get down, Holly," he ordered, facing her again.

She bit her lower lip, flashed him a look of beleaguered hatred and began to bounce again. Slowly. Defiantly.

It was giving David motion sickness. With a muttered curse, he grasped her and wrenched her down. She stumbled and fell against him—every day had its high point, he thought wryly—and then she righted herself, bunching up her fists and using them to thrust away from his chest.

"I was telling the truth when I said I loved you, Holly," he said, allowing her to keep the small distance she apparently needed, "so stop flaring your nostrils and clenching your fists and listen to me."

"You go straight to hell, Mr. Goddard!" she gasped out. "Or is it 'God' for short?"

David's jawline tightened painfully. "Dammit, Holly," he bit out, "can't you see that I was caught in this trap as much as you were? I came here to find out if you were helping Craig in any way and—"

"You mean you were spying on me, too? That you weren't just waiting for my brother to stumble into your net?" Holly could be shrill, but David loved her anyway. Though right now he wanted to turn her over his knee and blister her delightful rear end. That was unthinkable, of course, but he did take some comfort in the fantasy.

"The president-elect was afraid you might be helping Craig sell secrets, Holly," he said evenly.

"Howard thought I was some kind of female James Bond?" She was seething now, showing her teeth. God, even though she was mad as hell and sweating, she was magnificent. "I don't believe it!"

"Believe it," David said.

"You lied to me the whole time!"

"Not the whole time. I meant it when I said I love you."

"Get out of my house!"

David stood stock-still. "Don't you want to know what's going to happen to Craig now that he's been taken into custody?"

That stopped her. She stood stiffly, attentively, her eyes searching his face. "Yes," she said in a whisper. "David, will they hurt him?"

"You've been watching too many espionage movies. They'll debrief him—" He paused, holding up both hands to stay the frantic questions he saw brewing in her green-blue eyes. "That only means that they'll find out what he knows and what he's told the KGB, among other people he might have been dealing with. And then, because of the cocaine problem, they'll hospitalize him for a while. Whether or not he actually goes to prison will depend on a lot of factors that can't be determined right now."

"He was so afraid of being caught!"

David ached for Holly, wished that he dared take her into his arms and hold her. "Holly, being stopped was the best thing that could have happened to Craig. The cocaine alone would have killed him. And what was the situation doing to you? To Toby?"

She was gnawing at her lip again, her eyes bright with unshed tears. "I'm glad that Craig won't have to run anymore. I-I didn't realize how sick he was until he told me about the drug."

"I know," David said softly.

Holly stiffened, and her eyes flashed again. "I was going to turn him in myself, you know. I didn't need you to come here and pretend you loved me. I could have handled the situation."

"Could you, Holly? Do you have any idea how insidious cocaine addiction can be, what it can make a person do?"

He saw her tremble and knew she was bracing herself against him, against all he represented. In that instant, he accepted the fact that he'd lost her.

"Get out," she said. "And don't come back, David. Don't call and don't come to my classes."

"Your classes? Surely you're not going to teach this week—the press will be lying in wait for you, Holly. They'll eat you alive!"

"I can take care of myself," she said. And then she turned away and David didn't have the heart to turn her around to him again.

"I love you," he said gruffly. Then he drew a deep breath, struggled to control the burning in his eyes and left her. She switched the TV back on and climbed back onto the trampoline, bouncing with a vengeance.

As David passed through the kitchen, the housekeeper gave him a sympathetic look. He shrugged and without speaking opened Holly's back door to step out into a world that was never going to be quite the same again.

The moment David was gone, Holly sank to her knees on the trampoline, covered her face with both hands and let the sobs that had been scalding her throat have free reign. Claudette Colbert laughed merrily on the television screen, and Madge spoke softly from the doorway.

"Go after him, Holly. If you love that man, don't you let him get away. You'll be sorry all your life if you do."

Holly stopped crying and drew a deep breath. She would be sorry all her life that she'd *met* David Goddard, maybe, but she would never be sorry for sending him away. Damn his sneaky hide anyway. Let him go and use some other unsuspecting woman.

"I will not have that traitor mentioned under this roof again, Madge," she said, rising to her feet and dashing away her tears with the cuff of her jogging jacket. "If he calls or comes to the door, he is to be turned away. Do I make myself clear?"

There was a brief, tense silence. "Yes," Madge said finally, with resignation. "Clear enough."

Sorry that she'd had to speak so harshly to Madge, who had always been as good a friend as she was a housekeeper, Holly nevertheless left the room without apologizing. She went upstairs, stripped off her jogging suit and showered.

At seven o'clock, she got into her car and drove downtown to teach her fruitcake class. The reporters were there, just as David had warned they would be, but so were the students. By sheer force of will, Holly taught the class as usual, the only deviation being that she didn't stay to gather up and clean the baking pans and mixing bowls.

Later, at home, Holly steeled herself and played back the messages her machine had been recording all day. With one startling exception, the calls were from news reporters. As if in a daze, Holly sat down to listen to the surprisingly ordinary voice of the next president of the United States.

"Hello, Holly. This is Howard. I'm sorry about Craig and all the fuss the press is probably stirring up. Madge and I just wanted you to know that we hope you'll come to Washington for the shindig next month." Having said his piece, Howard hung up without another word and the tape was blank after that.

This is Howard...sorry about Craig...hope you'll come to Washington...The phrases echoed in Holly's overwrought mind and her broken heart. Maybe, just maybe, she would go to Washington. Maybe she would attend the balls and the parties and the swearing-in. Maybe she would tell Howard to his open and trustworthy face that she was just as loyal an American as the next person. "Do you solemnly swear," she imagined the Speaker of the House asking dear Howard, "that you will monitor the activities of your third cousin, the cookbook author, lest she undermine the security of this great country of ours?"

Howard, of course, would so swear.

Just then, Elaine arrived with Toby and, to Holly, she looked just a bit sheepish. Toby was carrying a dime-store fishbowl as though it were gold, frankincense or myrrh, and two goldfish hovered inside, staring stupidly.

"David gave me these," the little boy spouted before Holly could make any kind of comment at all. "He said I could take care of them for him, but I'm not s'posed to worry if they buy the farm 'cause they only cost seventy-nine cents a piece and they're spendable."

Expendable. Of course. The way Holly was expendable. The way Toby, though he hadn't made that painful discovery yet, was expendable. "Take the fish to your room, Toby," she said evenly.

When Toby was gone, she attacked an uncomfortable Elaine with, "You let David see Toby, didn't you? Why did you do that, Elaine, when you knew—"

"He only wanted to say good-bye!" Elaine broke in defensively. She looked pale and tired and a little harried, and Holly realized belatedly how hard this day had been for her friend.

"I'm sorry, Elaine. I shouldn't have jumped all over you that way."

Elaine managed a shaky smile. "We're all on edge, I suppose. I can't tell you how much I'm looking forward to putting on my old chenille bathrobe and curling up with Roy and a good book!"

Holly felt a touch of envy, somewhere in the deepest, darkest corner of her heart. Was she ever going to have anybody she could wear a chenille bathrobe in front of and "curl up" with?

It didn't seem very likely because she knew that she was never going to love a man the way she'd loved David Goddard. Never ever again.

"You can take the rest of the week off if you'd like," Holly offered in an unsteady voice.

"Not me," Elaine said, squaring her shoulders and trying to look intrepid. "I'm made of better stuff than that and so are you."

Holly smiled, even though tears were dangerously near the surface. "So you are. Thank you, Elaine, for everything."

Elaine hugged Holly briefly and patted her shoulder. "Anything for the boss," she said, and then she was leaving again, on her way home to Roy and the chenille bathrobe and a good book.

If Holly hadn't liked her friend so much, she would have hated her for being so lucky.

## Chapter Nine

Walt Zigman had seen that look before; it was a look that meant an agent had lost his spirit and maybe his grip. Damned shame it had to happen to a man like Goddard. He sat back in his desk chair and maneuvered his cigar stub from one side of his mouth to the other.

Goddard sat in the chair Walt knew the agents called the "hot seat," his long frame lank with an effort to hide tremendous pressure. "I told you she was clean," he said after a long, uneasy silence.

"Maybe you read palms or tea leaves, Goddard, but I don't. We had to know."

Goddard darted Walt a look meant to slice deep, and to Walt's surprise, it did. "Holly Llewellyn wasn't guilty of any crime. As far as I'm concerned, she's been harassed."

"Horsechips. She aided and abetted a suspected felon, Goddard. She's lucky we didn't bring her in, too."

Goddard was glaring now; his hands, gripping the arms of his chair, whitened at the knuckles. Though he hid the fact, Walt was pleased by the reaction; maybe this agent would be all right after all.

"Here." Goddard slapped a thin file folder down in the middle of a stack of memos and notes. Walt's whole life was one big memo these days, what with the transition from one administration to another and the inaugural festivities coming up in January. Security problems were everywhere and Walt Zigman didn't need another hassle.

"What's this?"

Goddard averted his eyes and shifted in his chair, but then he met Walt's gaze squarely. "My letter of resignation," he answered.

If there was regret in his voice, Walt didn't catch it. He wanted to swear. "You sure about this, Goddard? You're a good agent."

"I'm sure."

"What the hell are you going to do with your time, for Christ's sake? Walk dogs?"

Goddard made a visible attempt to keep his temper. "I'm qualified to practice law, in case you've forgotten."

"That little—that Llewellyn woman really got under your skin, didn't she?" Walt paused, sighed, lit the cigar stub and puffed industriously for a few moments. "Dammit, Goddard, we're swapping administrations here. We got an inaugural coming up in a little better than a month! I need every experienced agent I've got right now!"

Goddard was waving away the cigar smoke with one hand and Walt ground the stub out in an ashtray. "For what? Standing around in Saks while the new first lady tries on six hundred pairs of shoes?"

"You'll be assigned to the president himself, Goddard."

Goddard pointed one index finger toward the ceiling and spun it round and round in a contemptuous circle.

"Well, what the hell do you want?" Walt snapped, annoyed and a little insulted.

"I want out of the Service," David replied flatly. "I'll stay until after inauguration week is over, but I want the presidential assignments—no walking dogs. No strolls in the Rose Garden. It's strictly Oval Office and Air Force One, Walt, or I'm out of here."

"All right, all right, you're on presidential detail." Walt took up the folder Goddard had laid on his desk and extended it. "You keep this."

"You keep it," Goddard argued, standing up. "I meant it when I said I wanted out."

"What the devil do you plan to do after January?"

Goddard shrugged. "I told you, Walt. I intend to practice law."

Walt muttered a swearword and picked up the remains of his cigar again. "Take over for Erickson, then. He's got a root canal scheduled for this morning."

Goddard winced sympathetically. "Where?"

"In his mouth, dammit," Walt grumbled, tossing the folder containing his best agent's resignation letter into a deep drawer.

"I was asking where to find the president, Walt," came the strained and humorless response.

Walt didn't look up. "Oval Office," he bit out.

Holly was just getting through her days and nights, operating on automatic pilot, so to speak. She tried to see Craig, but he refused any contact with her or with her lawyer. Soon after that, he was transported to Washington, D.C. for the debriefing David had told her about.

It hurt, having to hear that on the evening news along with the rest of the world.

Christmas was fast approaching, though, and for Toby's sake, Holly tried her best to get into the spirit of things. She shopped, she baked, she decorated the house and put a wreath on the front door. But every time she so much as looked at the Christmas tree, she was filled with memories that brought tears to her eyes and a painful catch to her throat. David was gone, really gone. She knew because she had looked up his address in Elaine's records of the last cooking class and driven to his apartment.

Two college girls were living there now, and they couldn't tell Holly anything about David Goddard except that he must have had a dog because there were these "grungy" stains on the rug. Holly had turned away and gone blindly back to her car, sitting there in the parking lot for a full fifteen minutes with her forehead resting despondently against the steering wheel. She had already known that David had returned to his old life in Washington, D.C., so why was it such a crushing blow to find that strangers were living in his apartment? What would she have said to him if he had been there?

Holly hadn't known the answer to either question and now, kneeling on the floor of her own living room, struggling to wrap a last-minute gift for Toby, she still hadn't worked it all out.

The door bell rang, and Holly sniffled and dashed a stray tear from her cheek. Who could that be? After all, it was Christmas Eve, and nearly eleven o'clock at that.

She opened the door to find Skyler Hollis standing on the porch, looking uneasy and snow-dappled and rather earnest. For the space of a second, Holly had allowed herself the fantasy that David would be there in the glow of the porch light, and she hoped her disappointment didn't show.

"Sky," she said. "Come in."

"I hope you don't mind my coming by, Holly. I know it's late—"

Cautious because Skyler could be damnably persistent at times and because she didn't want to give him the wrong idea, Holly stepped back to admit him without saying anything.

He was carrying two beautifully wrapped packages in his arms. "I did my Christmas shopping last July," he explained. "I couldn't very well give Toby's to Mary Ann, so—"

Holly smiled because it was just like Skyler to do his Christmas shopping in July. He had probably addressed his cards then, too, though she hadn't received one. "Come in, Sky, and sit down. I think there might be some eggnog left."

He entered the living room ahead of her, put the two packages beneath the tree, then went to the hearth, ostensibly to examine Toby's as-yet-unfilled stocking, and confessed, "I've been worried about you, Holly, since that thing with your brother broke." He let the stocking fall back into place and turned to face her with the eyes of a concerned friend. "Are you all right?"

Holly shrugged and averted her gaze so that he wouldn't see the tears that had gathered there. "I'm all right," she lied.

"Toby?"

Toby was resilient. In fact, he was rather enjoying the notoriety of having a "spy" for a father. "Toby is okay, too, Sky. How have you been?"

A smile broke across his face, warm and, to Holly, very reassuring. "I'm dating Mary Ann," he said.

Holly was pleased and she hugged Skyler impulsively. "That's wonderful."

Skyler was still grinning. "I'm opening another store, too—up in Colville. I've been wanting to spend more time there."

Colville was a good-sized town and very near the farm. Holly smiled, starting to ladle out a cup of eggnog from the crystal bowl in the middle of the coffee table. Earlier, Roy and Elaine and Madge had all been by, and Holly had done her best to present them with some sort of celebration. "Your parents must be happy about that."

"Oh, none of that for me," Skyler said quickly, referring to the eggnog. "That stuff is fattening, you know."

Holly chuckled and took a sip from the cup herself. Lord knew, she spent so much time running on the mini-trampoline that she didn't have to worry about calories.

"You really ought to get away from Spokane for a while," Skyler said, watching her with a sort of gentle disapproval that implied she wasn't her usual self. "Hawaii, maybe, or—"

Holly laughed. "I can't go away, Skyler, much as I would like to. Toby is in school."

"All the same—"

She went to him, standing on tiptoe to plant a sisterly kiss on his cool, clean-shaven cheek. "Don't worry about me, Skyler. Please. I'm going to be just fine. You just concentrate on Mary Ann."

He returned her kiss, though her forehead was the target. "That guy is gone, isn't he?"

Holly's throat felt thick and sore again; she could only nod.

"He's a real fool," Skyler said. There was a long silence and then he started toward the door again, still wearing his coat. "I guess I'd better go," he said gruffly, his hand on the knob. "I've got a long drive to make."

"Be careful," Holly managed to say.

Skyler cleared his throat and nodded. When he met Holly's eyes, his gaze was full of something she had been getting too much of lately—sympathy. "I will. Merry Christmas, Holly."

Holly swallowed hard. "Merry Christmas, Skyler."

When he was gone, Holly walked back to the living room. The fire was burning low, the lights on the tree were glimmering and a Kate Smith Christmas carol was coming softly from the stereo. Holly swallowed again, squared her shoulders and methodically filled Toby's stocking until it bulged. For the first time in her entire life, she cried on Christmas Eve.

It seemed to Chris that her brother's smile was a little sad as he filled the girls' Christmas stockings and returned them to the hooks on the mantelpiece. He was looking at the two stockings that remained: his own and Chris's.

"I didn't know you still had these," he said gruffly.

Chris ached for him; though he hadn't said much about the disaster in Spokane, she knew David well enough to guess that he'd fallen for someone out there—probably Holly Llewellyn herself—and lost her. Her own painful divorce was two years in the past, but enough of the hurt lingered for her to sympathize.

"Holidays are the worst, aren't they?" she prompted softly, perching on the arm of the sofa and watching her brother.

David was tracing the letters of his name, awkwardly written in glitter across the top of the old, red-corduroy stocking. "Remember the year Mom made these, Chris? She was so proud of them."

Chris closed her eyes momentarily, scrounging up a smile. "You were Joseph in the church play," she recalled aloud. "Mom made your robe from an old sheet with the Lone Ranger all over it."

David laughed gruffly. "Yeah. You were an angel that year. Talk about miscasting." He fell silent, then turned to face his sister, his dark-blue eyes full of pain. "Do you miss Dennis?"

The truth was that Chris rarely thought of her ex-husband. She was too busy with her girls, the house, the cover designs she painted for romance novels. "At Christmas I get a little sentimental. Most of the time, I revel in how much he and Mona deserve each other."

David laughed again, and the pain in his eyes faded a little. "I think the same thing about Marleen and her monkeys," he confessed.

"Something is hurting you," Chris prompted gently, folding her arms.

"Being a two-time loser, I guess," came the hoarse admission.

"Holly Llewellyn?"

David lowered his handsome head. "Not much gets by you, does it, Chris? You ought to be an FBI agent or something."

"Walt's daughter tells me you're resigning."

David cursed, but with less spirit than Chris would have liked. "Zigman has a big mouth."

Boldly, Chris went to her desk, picked up the telephone in both hands and thrust it toward her brother. "Call Holly and wish her Merry Christmas," she said.

"It's too late—"

Chris glanced at the clock on the mantelpiece. "It's only eleven out there. I'll bet she's still up."

David considered the telephone for a moment, as though it were some complicated equation, then turned resolutely away. "Shall I bring the girls' presents in from the garage?"

Chris sighed. From long experience she knew how stubborn her brother could be. She set the phone back in its place. "Let me check and see if they're asleep yet. Sometimes they pretend."

"How do you know if they're pretending?" David asked, so guilelessly that Chris had to laugh.

"Men! You tickle them, of course. If they giggle, they're playing possum."

David shook his head, grinning. Because his eyes had strayed to the telephone, Chris turned quickly and hurried up the stairs and into her daughters' room. She remained there, in the darkness, long after discovering that they were both asleep.

The telephone was ringing. Holly stared at it over her shoulder, parts of the Ewok village she was trying to assemble still in her hands. She dropped a plastic palm tree and lunged for the receiver, telling herself that she mustn't let Toby be awakened by the noise.

"Hello?" she whispered, breathless with the foolish hope she couldn't seem to let go of.

Long-distance. The dull whir betrayed the call as long-distance. Holly's weary heart leaped within her.

"Hello?" she said again, because her caller seemed stumped for words.

"This is David," came the gruff, belated greeting.

Holly sagged onto the couch, dizzy with relief and with pain. "Oh," she said woodenly.

"Did I wake you?"

"N-No—I was putting out the Santa Claus things for Toby," Holly answered. Damn you, you should be here helping me, she added in her mind. For the moment, the fact that she had sent David away herself escaped her.

"How is Toby?"

God, the man was a conversational genius. Maybe that came from standing silent guard over presidents, ever-alert for any sort of danger. "He's doing okay," Holly replied. "He still has the fish."

"I hope their personalities have improved. They were definitely lackluster company when I had them."

Tears were streaming down Holly's face now, but they weren't audible, she hoped, in her voice. "What do you want from two goldfish? The old soft-shoe?"

David laughed. It was good to hear that sound, even if it was distant. "A medley of Elton John's greatest hits would have been nice."

"I'll buy them a little piano."

David's chuckle seemed to reach across the three thousand miles that separated them and caress Holly. "Have you forgiven me yet?"

"Quite honestly, no." It was sad to feel the anger again, the hurt. "Why concern yourself, David? You got your man and all that."

"It's my woman I'm concerned with."

Holly thrust out her chin, determined not to let him touch her with his voice. But she reddened to remember being his woman on that very couch and her body responded with a keen, embarrassing ache in her middle and a warm swelling in her breasts. "There are two college girls living in your old apartment," she said, and then hated herself for revealing that she'd gone there.

David must have sensed her discomfort, for he mercifully allowed the faux pas to pass. "Did they get the stains out of the rug?" he quipped.

Despite herself Holly laughed. "No. As a matter of fact, they didn't. They asked me if you had a dog."

There was a short, uncomfortable silence. "Holly," David finally ventured, "are you coming to Washington for the inauguration?"

Holly was winding and unwinding the phone cord around her finger. "I hadn't thought about it," she lied. The truth was that she had thought of little else; she'd been wondering if David would be at any one of the round of parties that were scheduled.

"Think about it."

"Why?"

"Dammit, you know why! Because I'll be in the president's hip pocket the whole time and I want to see you, that's why."

"Some Secret Service agent you are," challenged Holly hotly, flustered because he'd touched a nerve. "Do you always flirt with women while you're supposed to be protecting the chief executive?"

David sighed and it was a sound heavy with exasperation and strained patience. "I'll make time for you, don't worry."

"You're not going to make any kind of time, mister, so don't *you* worry!"

"Damn it all to hell, Holly, will you pull in your righteous indignation for one minute and listen to me?"

"No!" hissed Holly, remembering the lies, the pretense, the humiliation of finding out that she had been used. "You treated me like a...like a bimbo!"

He laughed. He actually had the gall, the temerity, to laugh!

"Merry Christmas!" Holly shouted and then she slammed the receiver back into its cradle.

After a few minutes spent wailing into a sofa pillow, Holly got hold of herself. She dried her tears and then stood up and went back to the Ewok village, putting it together carefully. When it was done, she made sure that the red wagon was at just the right angle beneath the tree and that the football was displayed to proper advantage.

Then she burrowed on her hands and knees through the scratchy, fragrant branches, to unplug the tree lights and plunge a conscientious finger into the base of the stand to make sure there was enough water.

Later, upstairs, she put on a nightgown, brushed her teeth, washed her face and stumbled off to bed. Regrettably, no sugarplums danced in her head—only memories of David trying to fly his funny-looking model airplane in the park, David mixing fruitcake batter in the department-store class, David ushering Elaine and Toby through a pressing crowd of reporters and cameramen. David making love to her.

"Nerd!" she whispered, pounding one fist into the pillow. "Get out of my mind!"

David remained in Holly's mind until she slept; then he haunted her dreams. It seemed she had barely closed her eyes before Toby was bouncing gleefully on her bed, his tightly filled Christmas stocking in hand.

"Look, Mom!" he crowed, holding up the evidence. "Santa Claus came!"

Holly widened her eyes in feigned wonder; it was a game they played every Christmas morning. In truth, Toby had already added Santa to his list of fictional characters, along with the Hardy Boys, Superman and the Tooth Fairy. He was still undecided about the Easter Bunny.

Toby upended the stocking and the booty spilled out over the quilt—an orange, a bottle of bubbles, a deck of trick cards, a candy cane and at least a dozen other things. His delight uplifted Holly as nothing else could have.

"Can we go downstairs and open the presents?" the child demanded once the stocking goodies had all been inspected and mentally categorized in order of usefulness.

Holly pretended to be surprised. "I think we should eat breakfast first," she said.

Toby caught her hand in his and literally dragged her out of bed, giving her only a second to scramble for her robe and slippers before proceeding out into the hall and down the stairs.

The next half hour was happily absorbed in ripping away paper and ribbons. Toby received a model car and a Scrabble game from Elaine and Roy, along with gifts from Holly herself, from Madge, from some of his friends at school. Skyler had given him a radio with—he was a true friend, that Skyler—earphones.

"Aren't you going to open any of your stuff?" he asked, surrounded by loot of every type. The eagerness in his eyes made her choose the package he and Elaine had wrapped in secret and put under the tree with a converse sort of ceremony.

"This one has been driving me crazy," she confessed, taking sidelong notes of the little boy's quick, delighted grin. She opened the parcel to find a book she had been longing to read tucked inside. And her pleasure was real.

After that, Holly uncovered an electric frying pan from Skyler—that made her smile—and a bottle of her favorite cologne from Elaine and Roy. There were other things, too, sent by her mother and faraway friends, but nothing, she assured the little boy, was quite as wonderful as the book he had chosen for her.

Toby was frowning, peering into the depths of the tree. "What's those things?" he asked.

"What things?" Holly asked, honestly puzzled.

"In there. There's two presents in there, in the branches!"

Holly smiled, thinking that Elaine must have hidden away an extra surprise or two for Toby. She liked to do things like that. "Guess you'd better investigate," she said.

Toby drew out a sizable box—Holly couldn't imagine how she had missed seeing it—and then a smaller one. Both were wrapped in gold foil.

"The big one's mine!" Toby crowed after reading the tag. He was already tearing at the wrapping as he extended the other present to a confused Holly.

She looked down at the tag on her own gift and her heart stopped, started again with an aching lurch. "Love, David," was written upon it in a typically firm hand.

Trembling just a little, Holly did not open her gift but, instead, watched Toby rip away a second layer of paper to reveal a plain box. Inside was a small robot, complete with hand-controls and a set of batteries.

Toby lifted round, shining eyes to Holly's face. "Who's this from?" he whispered, awed. It was obvious that he was considering shifting Santa Claus from the fiction list to the one peopled by Holly and his teachers and everyone else he could see and touch.

"From David, I think," Holly said, and thank heaven, Toby was too enthralled with the gift to notice the tremor in his aunt's voice.

"Wow," he said, dragging the word out for that emphasis peculiar to seven-year-old boys.

Holly's eyes were stinging a bit, and she averted her face for a moment before opening her own present with numb, awkward fingers. Inside was a small, elegant velvet box, and inside that was the most beautiful diamond engagement ring she had ever seen. Still trembling, Holly opened the note that had been rolled up and slipped through the ring itself. *"Marry me or I'll jump off the Washington Monument. Subtly, David."*

Holly couldn't help it. She laughed. She bit her lower lip to stop herself and that didn't help so she laughed again. Tears were streaking down her cheeks and Toby was looking at her in total confusion.

"What's-a-matter, Mom?" he asked, flushed with concern.

Holly closed the ring box firmly. "Nothing," she said. "Nothing is the matter."

"Was it a joke present?" Toby wanted to know, and his manner said that he wouldn't consider that untoward.

"Yes," Holly managed to say, taking the gift, box, wrapping paper and all, to the mantelpiece, where she tucked it behind a picture of her grandmother. Out of sight, out of mind, she told herself without much conviction.

All through that hectic day, all through the hurried breakfast, all through the drive to Elaine and Roy's apartment, all through Christmas dinner and the rousing trivia game that followed, Holly's mind and heart kept straying back to that ring and all it meant.

Of course, she couldn't marry David Goddard, as intriguing as the possibility was—not after what he had done. But she would take a certain pleasure in throwing that diamond in his face when she went to Washington next month to attend Howard's inauguration.

## Chapter Ten

Elaine was fairly dancing with excitement, her eyes bright and wide. She hugged Holly unreservedly, as other passengers pressed past them to board the airplane, and enjoined, "You have the best time anybody has ever had at an inauguration, Holly Llewellyn!"

Holly felt rueful and wary—perhaps it was a mistake to go to Washington after all—but she did return Elaine's hug. "Take care of Toby," she said.

"You know I will," Elaine scolded good-naturedly.

Holly wished she could back out at this late date but resigned herself to the fact that she couldn't. She squared her shoulders, drew a deep breath and entered the covered passageway leading to the airplane. She looked back once, wavering, but Elaine made a little shooing motion with her hands and winked encouragingly.

The flight was uneventful. Holly had a brief stop-over in Denver, and then it was on to Washington, where a car and driver were waiting to take her to the White House—was this really happening to her? As a relative of Howard's—good heavens, she barely remembered him—Holly was to be accommodated in style at 1600 Pennsylvania Avenue.

Escorted by a grim-looking Secret Service agent who would obviously rather not have been bothered, Holly was quickly shuffled into a limo with tinted windows and driven to the most august address in the United States.

On the way, she tried to make conversation with the agent who sat in the back with her. A little chit-chat, she thought, might ease her nervousness about what was to come. "Jimmy Carter came to Spokane once," she ventured, "to speak at Riverfront Park. He rode past in a car like this one, with darkened windows, and I think he smiled at me because I saw a flash of teeth."

The chauffeur chuckled to himself, though his eyes were fixed on the crazy Washington traffic. But the Secret Service man only reacted with a look that questioned her sanity. She supposed that Jimmy Carter and his teeth were old news to this guy, but he could have been a little friendlier all the same. Holly resisted an urge to tap on his forehead with her knuckles and ask if there was anybody in there.

They entered the White House grounds through a back gate, snow crunching beneath the limo's tires as it came to a stop at a rear door. Holly drew in her breath and let it out as a long, Tobylike, "Wow."

The Secret Service agent cleared his throat, got out of the car and extended a hand to Holly. Reluctantly, she accepted it. This character had no personality at all, it seemed. He was certainly nothing like David.

Holly left the limo with as much dignity as she could summon. Perhaps David would behave in just this manner when he was on duty; for better or worse, she was about to find out.

In a small anteroom—Holly had no way of knowing what part of this fabled mansion they were in—another agent appeared. Like the first one, he wore a trim three-piece suit, a no-nonsense expression and a very small earphone that probably connected him to all sorts of small in-house intrigues.

Holly was more nervous than ever, and that made her chatter again. "George Washington actually slept here," she muttered, wide-eyed.

The agents exchanged a long-suffering look, probably thinking how unfortunate it was that the president-to-be had to have such a bumpkin for a cousin. "This way, Madam," one of them said, and Holly found herself being propelled through a series of rooms and up a rear staircase.

"Do you know David Goddard?" Holly tried again. Maybe these guys were at least semi-human.

The agents traded another look. Apparently the answer to that question was a state secret, for neither of them bothered to respond.

They were now on the floor where the first family resided. Holly decided charitably that that accounted for the reticence of the two men escorting her. She was deposited in a lovely room decorated all in blue. To her amazement, her baggage had already been brought up, and a small, plump woman in a maid's uniform was busy taking Holly's new evening gowns from the garment bag and hanging them carefully in the closet.

Here, perhaps, was a human being, though after the Secret Service agents, Holly didn't want to make any rash judgment.

"Hello," she ventured.

Tha maid, an elderly woman with a look of long service about her, smiled warmly. "Hello, Ms. Llewellyn. And welcome to Washington."

"Thank you," Holly said with a sigh of relief.

"I'm Mrs. Tallington, and I'll be helping you while you're with us. The first lady asked me to tell you that she will be in to greet you shortly."

So, Holly thought, Howard's Maggie is already referred to by that lofty title, even though the swearing-in isn't until tomorrow. "Have you worked here for a long time?" she asked as Mrs. Tallington examined Holly's blue chiffon, made a cluck-clucking sound and shook her gray head.

"Since FDR and Eleanor," came the brisk answer. "They come and they go. Some are happier to leave than to arrive, I might add. This gown will need pressing."

Holly chuckled and relaxed enough to set her purse on a mahogany dresser and remove her winter coat. "I was afraid everyone here would be like those men who brought me upstairs."

A mischievous light twinkled in Mrs. Tallington's bright blue eyes. Her snow-white hair made a little knot on the top of her head, just visible through the gauzy fabric of her cap. "Don't speak ill of those who are probably standing right outside your door," she warned good-naturedly.

Drawing in a quick breath, Holly went to the door, opened it a crack and peered out. The two agents looked back at her impassively, and she closed the door again with a resolute click.

Mrs. Tallington was chuckling. "A little unnerving, isn't it? But they're there to guard you; they mean you no harm. Just make yourself comfortable and pretend they're not around."

Holly had never been "guarded" before, and she was nonplussed. Once again she had misgivings about the wisdom of coming here, to this place where she didn't belong, where everything was so formal and intimidating.

"I'd like to see the room where Mr. Lincoln slept," she said to distract herself.

Mrs. Tallington nodded, her eyes twinkling again, toward a huge painting of the Great Emancipator himself. "You're in it," she replied matter-of-factly. "Some say they've seen Abe sitting on the edge of that very bed, taking off his shoes."

Holly shuddered despite her pleasant surprise at finding herself in a room once occupied by one of the greatest men in history. She certainly hoped that Mr. Lincoln would not deign to sit upon the side of the bed while she was in it—that would be most disconcerting.

There was a slight ballyhoo outside and then a knock at the door. Before Holly could issue any sort of invitation, Maggie swept into the room, all campaign-trail smiles, her glistening blond hair artfully coiffed, her dress a designer original.

"Holly, dear! How marvelous to see you!"

Holly stiffened, then worked up a smile. After all, this was Lincoln's bedroom and this was the first lady of the land. Such things had to be accorded due respect. "Hello, Maggie," she said.

Maggie bypassed Holly's cheek with a distant-cousin-by-marriage kiss. "Howard and I are so pleased that you could come!"

Mrs. Tallington, the wrinkled blue chiffon evening gown draped over one capable arm, ducked out of the room without a word. Holly watched her go, using the time to overcome her secret ire over what Howard and his suspicions had put her through.

The first lady drew back her guest's attention with a trilling, musical laugh. "Howard will apologize himself, of course," she said, "but I did want to tell you that we're both very sorry over what happened to poor Craig."

Holly was momentarily annoyed. They were very sorry. Did they think their third cousin from Spokane had come down in the last snowstorm? They had believed, actually believed, that Holly could turn on her own country. "Thank you," she forced herself to say.

Maggie dragged discerning eyes over Holly's rumpled woolen suit. "You'll want to change before meeting with the president, of course."

"Which president?" Holly wanted to ask, but she bit the perverse inclination back. The outgoing administration was probably out-gone anyway. "Of course," she answered.

Maggie smiled her blinding, trust-my-husband smile. "Wonderful. When you're ready, just tap at the door and the men stationed outside will see you to the Oval Office."

The Oval Office. Holly's knees weakened and she hoped she didn't sway visibly. Me? she thought. In the Oval Office?

Maggie noted with a glossy smile that her guest was properly overwhelmed by the magnitude of it all. With a cheery word of farewell, she swept out.

Holly wobbled her way into the bathroom that must have been added on sometime after Mr. Lincoln's demise, undressed and ran a hot bath. Half an hour later, she was presentable again, her hair neatly brushed, her makeup fresh. Wearing an expensive suit of beige and emerald, she drew a deep breath and tapped at the door, as instructed.

It opened to give Holly Llewellyn the shock of her life. David Goddard was smiling down into her face. "That outfit makes you look like a mid-Western schoolmarm," he muttered out of one side of his mouth.

Holly grappled inwardly for composure, then lifted her chin and retorted, "If it was good enough for Merv Griffin, buddy, it's good enough for Howard."

For a moment, before the intangible veil of officialdom fell over his eyes, making them expressionless, David allowed them to transmit a welcome that made Holly pinken slightly.

She was led to the Oval Office itself. There were marines guarding the double doors, and beyond that point, there was a spacious outer office, populated by secretaries and advisors of various stations. One of them pressed a button on an intercom and said, "Mr. President, Ms. Llewellyn has arrived."

It was unsettling, the way everyone around there seemed to know Holly's name without her telling them. Did they know how much she owed on her charge cards and what kind of hairspray she used and whether or not her library books were overdue, too?

She flung one scathing, sidelong look at David, remembering just how personal a presidentially ordered investigation could get. "Rat," she whispered, and one side of David's firm mouth twitched almost imperceptibly.

"Send her in, send her in!" boomed Howard's jovial voice over the intercom.

Holly was escorted right to the doors—what did they think she was going to do? Bolt and run? Make a stirring speech in favor of the Kremlin, Mom and borscht?

"Let go of me!" she hissed.

Both agents immediately released their hold on her elbows. Though his face was completely expressionless, David's mouth twitched again and something danced in the blue depths of his eyes. "Give 'em hell, Llewellyn," he said, to the other agent's obvious distress.

And then Holly was inside that office of offices, alone except for Howard, and she couldn't hide her reaction to it all. After all, this was a place where dramatic decisions had been made. John F. Kennedy had discussed the Cuban missile crisis with Bobby. FDR had planned the New Deal. Abe Lincoln had listened to the ominous beat of Confederate drums from just across the Potomac....

"Wow," she said.

Howard, a genteel-looking, gray-haired man with a powerful build and a winning smile, stood up in gentlemanly deference. "My sentiments exactly," he said. "Actually, I'm just getting the feel of the place myself. This isn't my office yet."

Holly liked Howard for saying that. "Your predecessor—?"

"He's around somewhere," Howard said. "We both want the transition to go as smoothly as possible and the president has been decent about this whole thing."

Howard gestured toward a long, comfortable-looking sofa, only one of several in the massive, overwhelmingly significant room, and Holly sat down gratefully.

"Tell me," she began, relaxing in the face of her cousin's easy, unofficial manner, "is the red phone really red?"

Howard laughed. "There it is, on the desk, the one on the left."

The telephone was ivory. Another legend shot to hell, thought Holly with a grin. But her grin faded as she considered the tremendous burdens that were about to be placed on this man's sturdy shoulders.

Howard had apparently guessed what she was thinking. "I'll do my best," he promised quietly and with conviction.

Holly's respect for the man deepened. "Waking up every morning, being responsible for much of the free world—I don't think I could do that."

The future president chuckled. "I can't make a decent wonton, so I guess we're even." He paused and cleared his throat in an I'm-about-to-say-something-momentous way. "Holly, Maggie and I are both very sorry about that investigation and the trouble it must have caused you."

Maggie's apology had been somewhat varnished and breezy, in Holly's opinion, but Howard's came across as the real thing. "You certainly had reason to doubt Craig," she admitted with dignity, "and I suppose you had no way of knowing that I would never take part in such a thing.''

Howard watched her with kindly, rather tired eyes. ''Thank you, Holly.''

Holly bolted to her feet, conscious of the drains on this man's time and energy. She didn't want to be one of them; he had important things to do. ''I'd better go and let you get back to your work. Do you think I could look around a bit?'' She paused and chuckled nervously. ''It isn't every day that a cookbook author from Spokane finds herself in the White House, you know.''

''Nor a lawyer from Oregon,'' quipped Howard, referring, of course, to himself.

Holly cocked her head toward the sturdy double doors and lowered her voice to a conspiratorial whisper. ''Do those two goons have to be on my heels the whole time?'' It felt good to refer to David Goddard as a ''goon,'' unsuitable as the word might be for such a smooth operator.

Howard laughed his loud, ingenuous laugh. ''I'm afraid so, Holly. They go with the territory.''

''You mean, the whole time I'm in Washington—''

''The whole time you're in Washington,'' confirmed Howard with resignation.

Holly shook her head in irritated wonder and laid her hand on a knob touched by some of the greatest—but she wasn't going to ride that mental train again. Presidents, as had just been brought home to her, were as human as anybody else. Still, it was exhilarating to venture among such illustrious ghosts.

David was waiting, sans his partner, just beyond the doors. ''I'd like a tour, please,'' she said, delighting in the brief flicker of irritation that moved in his eyes and tightened his splendid jawline a little.

They spent the rest of the morning visiting various parts of the White House, some accessible to tourists, some private. David might have been a stranger, so clipped were his explanations of this painting and that chair, and Holly told herself that it was just as well. After what he had done to her, who wanted intimate conversation?

She did. But she did a commendable job of hiding her disappointment at David's formal, distant manner.

It wasn't until he brought her back to Mr. Lincoln's bedroom that he said anything unagentlike, and even that was brief because the two men assigned to stand outside Holly's door and look intimidating were already zeroing in.

"I'm off duty at seven," he intoned. "Meet me outside the tourists' entrance."

"I will not—"

David was turning away. Damn, but he looked magnificent in his navy-blue, don't-mess-with-me-I-guard-presidents suit. "Be there," he tossed back in parting.

Holly dodged inside her room and closed the door, impotently furious. The thing that made her maddest of all was knowing that even if it meant missing dinner with Maggie and Howard, she would be at the tourists' entrance at seven sharp.

David was pacing. He stopped occasionally to glare at his watch. Holly so enjoyed his discomfiture that had it not been for the two suits walking within lunging distance of each of her elbows, she would have hidden behind a statue and watched for a while.

"You're relieved," he said bluntly, his eyes darting from one impassive Secret Service face to the other.

"You got clearance for this, Goddard?" dared the taller one.

"Call upstairs and ask if you don't believe me," was David's response to the challenge.

If this was a bluff, the "goons" were calling it. One of them muttered something into the little device that curved around the side of his cheek, his eyes never leaving David's face. Good heavens, Holly reflected, they don't even trust each other!

There was a buzzing sound, the response being discernible only if you happened to be wearing one of those communication contraptions, which, of course, Holly wasn't.

"You're clear, Goddard."

David's jawline tensed, then relaxed again. Was it possible that he found all this cloak-and-dagger stuff just as tiresome as Holly did? "Gee, thanks, Ranford," he bit out. And then as he pulled Holly into the protective curve of one arm, he added, "Don't wait up for us."

Holly found herself being ushered outside into the icy, snow-laced Washington wind and across a slippery parking lot. "Will they?" she asked, glancing back over one shoulder.

David opened the passenger door of a small green sports car and hustled her into the seat. "Will they what?"

Holly waited until he was behind the wheel before replying impatiently, "Will they wait up for us?"

David laughed. "No. They'll follow us. They'll sit across the street from my apartment building until we come out and then they'll tail us back to Pennsylvania Avenue. At which time they will collect you at the rear entrance and muscle you upstairs to your room. Neither of them will draw a calm breath until you're tucked in, safe and sound."

"I don't want to go to your apartment—"

David's perfect teeth flashed in the relative darkness. "Too bad," he replied.

"A lot of damned good it does to have bodyguards!" Holly spouted, unnerved but tingly at the prospect of being alone with David Goddard. Distinctly tingly.

David only laughed. At the gate, he stopped to show his ID and the guard peered in, taking a long, level look at Holly.

"Do they always make such a big fuss about every little move a person makes?" Holly demanded, looking back as a limo followed them out, the gate slamming shut behind.

"Yes," David sighed. And he sounded tired and exasperated.

As they drove through the dark, snow-dusted streets of Washington and into an area Holly recognized as Georgetown, she glanced back at their one-car entourage and sighed, "Nobody will ever accuse those guys of being subtle. How do you stand it, David?"

"Stand it? I've done it myself a thousand times."

"Followed people? Who?"

"People who were taking a president's daughter out on a date, for one example."

He maneuvered the car into an underground parking area beneath one of the historic, renovated houses Holly had heard and read so much about. To hide her sudden case of jangly nerves, she sat up very straight in the seat and said, "This is quite an expensive car.

It's good to know that civil servants are so well compensated for their work.''

David grinned at her sarcasm, apparently unaffected by it. ''Wait until you see my apartment,'' he baited her.

Holly was scowling as he parked the car and came around to collect her. As they hurried toward an elevator, she could hear the rhythmic click-click of the agents' shoes behind them. ''They're not making any effort to be quiet, are they?''

''Why should they? They know that we know they're there.''

''I thought you said they would sit outside, in the car,'' fretted Holly, looking back over one shoulder.

David thrust her into the elevator the moment the doors opened and took obvious delight in the fact that his colleagues were summarily shut out. ''They'll stand outside my door for a while just to make sure we're not up to anything—'' he paused, winking in a way that made Holly flush with quiet outrage ''—unAmerican.''

Holly gave him an arch look. ''Why don't you just tell them that you've already checked me out, Agent Goddard?''

The man was impossible. Instead of getting mad, he laughed and said, ''I've missed you, you tart-tongued little wench.''

Holly bristled. ''Tart-tongued little what?''

They had reached David's floor, the elevator doors whisking open to reveal an expensively carpeted hallway. He avoided answering by catching her hand in his and pulling her up to a door marked 17B.

It turned out to be a place that would raise the hackles of any taxpayer. The carpets were lush, the furniture was sturdy and obviously antique, and the lighted paintings on the walls had not come from the housewares department at K-Mart. One of them, unless Holly was mistaken, looked like a Picasso.

A lulling, bubbling sound came from everywhere and Holly saw that there were no less than four sizable aquariums in the living room, every one of them populated by expensive tropical fish. The effect was quietly exotic.

Holly turned to David, desperately stalling, wondering why she had allowed him to bring her here at all. "You are overpaid, Mr. Goddard," she accused.

He laughed and touched her nose with a winterchilled index finger. "Before you lodge an official complaint, may I say in my defense that my grandfather owned a large farm in Nebraska, and furthermore, that when it was sold at his death, I inherited half the money?"

Holly sagged a bit, tired and at a loss, but then rallied with a challenging, "Who got the other half?"

David's eyes danced and he grinned. "My sister, Chris. Are you disappointed?"

"Why would I be?"

He was easing her coat from her shoulders, and as ordinary as that gesture was, it seemed strangely sensual then. "I think you were hoping to add philandering to my other crimes. Be honest, Holly—for just a moment, you thought I was married, didn't you?"

The thought had crossed her mind. After all, if David would lie about his occupation and his feelings for her, he might have lied about his marital status, too. "I considered it. Then I realized that no woman in her right mind would ever put up with you."

Having laid her coat aside, David went to a beautifully carved bar and began rattling bottles and glasses about with a decorum suited to his surroundings. "Would you like something to drink?"

A drink might steady her nerves, Holly thought. Then again, it might lead her to make a fool of herself. "White wine, please," she said primly, seated now on a plush sofa of navy blue suede.

He brought the wine, holding a mixed drink of some sort in his other hand, and sat down, not on the couch beside Holly, but on a matching hassock nearby. Introspectively, David studied the amber depths of his glass.

"What did you think of your Christmas present?" he asked gruffly, still avoiding her eyes.

Reminded, Holly opened her purse and brought out the present in question, settling the small velvet box on the coffee table. "I think you shouldn't have given it to me," she replied coolly.

She ached at seeing his strong shoulders stoop just slightly. "My timing was less than perfect, I guess," he reflected, at length.

"Considerably less," Holly said softly, hurting because it was obvious that David did. "But Toby liked his robot."

Indigo eyes searched her face. "Holly, give me one more chance. Just one."

Holly tightened both hands around her wineglass, as though it could anchor her, enable her to ride out the emotional storm that was coming. "I didn't come to Washington so I could see you again, David," she said. And it was only after the words were out of her mouth that Holly realized she was lying.

## Chapter Eleven

Are you hungry?'' David's question broke the uncomfortable silence.

Holly had eaten aboard the airplane but that, of course, had been some hours before. "A little."

David laughed, but it was a ragged sound, humorless and painful to hear. "God knows who you might have rubbed elbows with tonight if you hadn't come with me. The least I can do is take you to the best restaurant in town."

"No," Holly said quickly, glancing apprehensively at the door. "I don't want those men watching every lift of my fork." Or following me to and from the rest room, she added to herself.

David stood up to remove his suit coat. Nestled ominously against his broad chest was a holstered pistol. "Sorry," he said hoarsely, catching Holly's look of horrified surprise.

She looked away, reminded once again of all the things that stood between them, then heard the brisk click of a drawer and what she thought was the turning of a key.

"I make a mean omelete," David offered in a low voice.

Holly forced her eyes back to him, and to her abject relief, the gun was gone. She managed a shaky smile. "I hope it's better than your fruitcake," she ventured, and this time, David's responding chuckle was warm and real.

He executed a sweeping bow, reminiscent of a continental waiter. "This way, Madam," he said.

Against her better judgment, Holly rose from the sofa and followed him through a small, formal dining room and into the kitchen. There was a butcher block table in the center of the room, and copper kettles hung from a black wrought-iron rack above that. The stove and sink were both within easy reach.

"Pretty nice," Holly approved, since she knew kitchens if she knew anything at all.

"Don't be too impressed," David warned with a half smile as he rolled up the sleeves of his white shirt and then went to the sink to wash his hands. "I wouldn't know an egg timer from hollandaise sauce. I only bought all this stuff to please my housekeeper."

"Is there anything I can do to help?" Holly asked, torn between attaching herself to this man like a barnacle and bolting out of the apartment on a dead run. The depths of her feelings for him were truly frightening; she had to remind herself that a relationship between them could never work.

"Yes," David responded, bringing an armload of ingredients from the fancy refrigerator, which had a sliding, opaque door. "Sit down at the table and relax."

Instead Holly claimed one of three high stools at the luncheon bar. There were louvered doors beyond them, opening into the dining room. She fixed her attention on the elegant refrigerator and tried to imagine it covered with memos and samples of a little boy's artwork. She couldn't, and that saddened her.

David's hands were busy chopping scallops crisp enough to appears in a *Bon Appetit* layout, but his eyes scanned Holly's face with a sort of weary tenderness. "You look as though you might just fall asleep in my culinary triumph," he observed.

Holly had no intention of falling asleep anywhere but in Mr. Lincoln's bedroom. "I'm all right," she said but an involuntary yawn belied her words.

David grinned and shook his head, moving on from the scallops to a mound of mushrooms. "Whatever you say," he replied.

Holly felt a blush rise in her face; it revived her a little, stinging the way it did. "I'm wide awake," she insisted.

He stopped slicing mushrooms, bracing himself against the block table with his hands. "What do you think I'm going to do, Holly? Pounce on you if you so much as close your eyes?

That made Holly laugh, however reluctantly. That was exactly what she'd thought, she realized. And it was a ridiculous notion. "I'm sorry," she said.

David went back to the project at hand, grinning mysteriously to himself. Holly would have given her Cordon Bleu diploma to know what he was thinking, but she was wise enough not to ask. Instead she just watched, yawning periodically, as David whisked eggs into a foamy froth, browned the scallops in butter, added the mushrooms and eggs at just the right moment.

They ate in the dining room, by candlelight, saying little. And good as the food was, Holly nearly disgraced herself by nodding off over her plate.

Exactly how it happened, and this was a very momentous "it," all things considered, was something that would always elude Holly. All her jet lag, all the rigors of the past couple of months, suddenly caught up with her. The room seemed to darken and the candlelight undulated and then David's arms were beneath her, strong and secure.

Holly yawned and made some senseless remark and David laid her gently down on a water bed. The waves lulled her further. "I can't...this isn't...Howard and Maggie..."

"Hush," he said, laying his fingers to her mouth and covering her with a satiny comforter.

"But—"

"Just sleep. As the president's cousin, you have a big day tomorrow. I'll make sure you're at the Capitol Building in plenty of time."

It was madness, but Holly believed him. And she was simply too tired to rally herself and get up off that swaying, lulling water bed. "It must have been...the wine..."

David chuckled and his lips touched her forehead, just briefly. "That and enough emotional trauma to devastate Mr. T. Sleep, sweetheart."

And Holly slept. She awakened a couple of hours later, confused and disoriented. When she remembered that she was in David Goddard's apartment, that the two agents assigned to her were probably still outside and coming to all sorts of scandalous conclusions, she sat bolt upright and gasped aloud.

It was a moment before she realized that David was not in the bed with her; when she made the discovery, Holly was both relieved and disappointed. "David?" she whispered, swinging her legs over the side of the bed. She was still completely dressed except for her shoes. "David?"

When there was no answer, she rose, not bothering to turn on a lamp, and groped her way out of the room. The living room beyond was dimly lit, but empty.

"David?" she ventured again. A small, cherry-wood grandfather clock chimed three times. Good Lord, how was she going to explain this to the Secret Service, to Howard and Maggie? "David!" she yelled.

He materialized, a man made of shadows, at the end of the hallway. His hair was rumpled, his eyes were glass and his chest was bare. Holly didn't dare look any lower. "What?" he yawned.

"Take me back to the White House this minute! My God, what those men must be thinking—"

"'Those men' were called off hours ago. Go back to bed, Holly."

Go back to bed? Was the man insane? "May I point out that it is three o'clock in the morning? My reputation is at stake here!"

David yawned again and stretched his arms above his head and the play of the all too masculine muscles in his shoulders and naked torso unsettled Holly all the more. "Right. Three o'clock. Your reputation," he mumbled.

Holly glared at him for a moment. "The agents really left?"

"Yes."

"How did you manage that, may I ask?"

"I told them you and I were going to spend the night making love."

Holly flushed. "You didn't!"

"Oh, yes I did. And what they don't know won't hurt them. You're not the only one with a reputation to maintain."

"Very funny! Take me home this instant."

"I'm going back to bed. I would recommend, Ms. Llewellyn, that you do the same. If you don't, I may forget my good manners and —"

A jolt went through Holly's just-awakened system, and it wasn't an unpleasant one. "And what?"

"Don't ask." He turned to leave her, there in the middle of his living room.

"I'll take a cab!" she threatened in a high-pitched voice. "I mean it, David Goddard..."

Her announcement trailed off when he suddenly whirled on his heels and came toward her, an evil, teasing look in his eyes. "That's it," he said. "I warned you."

Holly trembled as he lifted her effortlessly into his arms. She should struggle. She should walk out. She should go down to the street and hail a cab. But she could do none of those things. She couldn't even speak.

David carried her back into the room where she had been sleeping only minutes before, stood her on her unsteady feet and began to undress her. "Maybe there is one way, lady, to convince you that I love you."

He removed the prim blouse and skirt she had changed into to meet him earlier, tossing each garment casually aside. Holly stood speechless before him in her camisole and her tap-pants, overcome by the feelings she had been struggling against ever since Craig's arrest.

Her head fell back as David bared her breasts and caressed them, his thumbs chafing the nipples until they stood out in eager surrender. Simultaneously, she trembled and sighed.

Presently David removed the camisole entirely, as he had her other clothes, flinging it aside. And then her tap-pants were sliding down over her quivering hips and thighs and they were gone, too.

"David," she choked in sweet desperation as he continued to caress her, more freely now, and with a boldness that made Holly ache to submit.

Finally he kissed her and if Holly Llewellyn had not been lost before, she was lost then.

David drew back from her mouth with obvious reluctance and muttered, "I must be the world's biggest fool—"

"Second biggest," Holly struggled to say as he placed her upon the water bed and joined her there. Then he began doing the most delicious, wicked things to her.

He drew sweet nectar from her breasts, he touched and stroked her, mastering her in ways that exalted, ways that soothed. And he brought her to a soaring preliminary release that left her quivering like a string, unable to see and nearly unable to breathe.

David entered her gently, with a low groan and an urgency as old as the stars. In the ensuing minutes, Holly quite literally lost her mind, groping for it as explosions of shattering joy shook her, finding it in her own cries of release and in David's.

Holly's face was hot, but she kept her eyes straight ahead as her personal Secret Service contingent escorted her through the rear part of the White House and right to the door of Mr. Lincoln's bedroom.

Inside, she rested her back against the heavy, carved wooden panels and struggled to catch her breath and cool her flaming cheeks with hands still icy from the frigid weather outside.

Mr. Lincoln observed her pensively from within his costly frame.

"I couldn't help it, Abe! I'm crazy about the man!" Holly hissed defensively as she stomped into the bathroom, peeled off yesterday's clothes and ran herself a deep, hot bath.

By inauguration time, Holly was dressed again, her hair and makeup done to perfection. Nothing of the abandon of the night before showed in her face—she hoped.

Holly rode to the Capitol Building in a limo, as a part of a long motorcade.

"Sure is a cold day for standing outside," observed the chauffeur.

Holly was grateful for his attempt at conversation, for she needed something else to think about besides the way she had tossed and writhed in David Goddard's bed the night before. It didn't help that he'd drawn that damned veil down over his eyes the moment he had deposited her in the waiting hands of her bodyguards. That had been so impersonal, so cold, and Holly's pride was still stinging. "I'll be glad when it's over," she sighed. "Isn't that terrible? I mean, this is an historic occasion and everything."

"It is that, Ma'am," replied the driver kindly. "A historical day and all that, I mean. But that don't change the fact that it's cold as the devil's heart out there."

The Secret Service agents sitting on either side of Holly were a different set than she'd had the day before, but they were just as dour and silent. Thank God the driver wasn't intimidated by their presence.

"No," said Holly. "It don't."

That deliberate slip of grammar brought a look from one of the agents, anyway. Holly thought she saw a grin peer out from behind the rim of his retina, though it disappeared, of course, in less than a moment.

Reaching the crowded Capitol Building, Holly and her escorts left the car. A microphone had been set up at the top of the fabled steps, along with a canopy of sorts and a number of folding chairs. Maggie and Howard were nowhere in sight, though there were hundreds of guests milling about in the chill of that day, Secret Service agents moving among them. They were easy to spot, not only because of their conservative suits and their earphones, but because their eyes moved constantly, searching every face, noting the rise of any arm.

When Howard and Maggie arrived, closely followed by the majority leader, they were surrounded by a bevy of agents, David among them. Like the others, he scanned the crowd incessantly, and Holly shivered, not because of the biting cold but because she knew in that instant that he would lay down his life for the president without hesitation. Just as promptly, he would take the life of anyone who was so foolish as to attempt an attack.

Holly barely heard the swearing-in itself; she was too busy watching David and trying to solve the mysteries he personified. She had every respect for his dedication to his job, of course, but it was very difficult to reconcile this cold-eyed man with the one who had made such thorough, gentle love to her the night before.

Tears of hopelessness began to burn behind Holly's eyes and ache in her sinuses. Like a fool, despite everything, she had entertained a fantasy or two concerning David Goddard and the future they might have together. Now, standing in the brutal wind, she had reality to deal with; David was always going to be the man who had come into her life as a liar, a pretender, an imposter. He was a man who wore a gun under his jacket, a man who would kill if he deemed it necessary.

Holly shivered again and clapped with numb hands as the new president lowered his right hand and turned to say a few words to the crowd. She didn't hear a word he said, so intent was she on David's immobile, watchful face. How could she have considered living with him, loving him for the rest of her life? Even if all the other problems could have been solved, there was still the ominous fact that he could be killed or crippled at any time. His work was dangerous.

"I'd like to leave now," Holly said to the agent standing at her right side. Without making any verbal response, he took her elbow in a firm hand and ushered her back to one of a dozen waiting limousines.

Safe in her room again some twenty minutes later, after declining an offhand, rushed invitation from Maggie to attend a state luncheon, Holly collapsed onto her bed with a pulsing headache.

Presently, Mrs. Tallington appeared with a tray and a look of sympathy. "Do you need a doctor, Madam?" she inquired.

Holly closed her eyes. She had taken two aspirin before lying down and she hoped they would be sufficient. "No, thank you," she said. "I'll be fine if I just rest a while."

"Eating a little something might help," imparted the veteran, and then she was gone.

When Holly could sit up without feeling queasy, she inspected the contents of her tray. Beneath aged, mellow silver covers were generous servings of creamed crab, mixed vegetables and warm, crusty bread.

Knowing the wisdom of what Mrs. Tallington had said, she forced herself to eat, though most of the portions were larger than she could have handled even if she'd felt her best.

She slept—her dreams were damnably erotic replays of the night before—and when she awakened there were lengthy shadows in the room and the tray had been taken away. Her blue chiffon, pressed to meet Mrs. Tallington's impeccable standards, hung from a peg on the closet door.

Holly wished she had the nerve to thrust that gown and all her other clothes into her suitcases and make a dash for the airport. That would be so much easier than facing David again!

But she couldn't bring herself to do it. The biggest of all the inaugural balls was to be held that evening, and Holly was enough of an adventuress to really want to attend. After all, she would probably never have a chance to do anything like that again.

Holly took another long, leisurely, scented bath, washed and dried her hair, carefully painted her nails.

She was wearing only a towel when the telephone at her bedside jangled, startling her so much that she jumped and had to clasp the towel in place again.

"Hello?"

"Holly, this is Howard. The staff tells me that you're a little under the weather."

Holly sighed, feeling troublesome and out of place. "I'm fine, Mr. President. Honestly. I think I was just a little tired."

"'Mr. President', is it?" Howard chuckled. "Well now, Holly, I like the sound of that, but I'm still just Howard to you."

Still just Howard. Grinning, Holly shook her head in wonder but said nothing, waiting for her illustrious caller to go on.

"I've arranged for you to meet with Craig first thing tomorrow morning, Holly. He's ready to talk with you now."

Holly's knees went weak and she sank to the edge of the bed. "C-Craig? He's here?

"He's at Walter Reed for the time being. Do you want to see him, Holly?"

Her throat tightened, memories of another Craig swirling in her mind: a laughing, responsible, healthy Craig. A devoted big brother. "Oh, yes," she said softly. "Yes, I want to see him."

"Good. We'll send you over there in a car, bright and early. In the meantime, young lady, you put on your dancing shoes and prepare to have yourself a good time at the shindig tonight."

Holly chuckled, though there were tears swimming in her eyes. "Being in the White House, going to an inaugural ball—I think I should wear glass slippers instead of dancing shoes."

"Can't dance in glass slippers," Howard retorted immediately. "You save a waltz for your old third cousin from Oregon, now."

"I will," Holly promised, and Howard rang off in his politely abrupt way.

Slowly, she set the receiver back in its cradle, drew a deep breath and went to the closet to find the special, strappy shoes she bought to wear with the blue chiffon. Turning one in her hand, Holly reminded herself that she was not Cinderella and that Howard was certainly not Prince Charming.

No, if Prince charming attended the ball at all, he would be wearing an earphone and a look fit to freeze-dry coffee beans.

The ballroom glittered with crystal chandeliers and silver punch bowls and guests one couldn't hope to encounter even on *The Merv Griffin Show*. Holly spotted David almost immediately and spent the next fifteen minutes trying to ignore him.

The orchestra played and Holly danced with a pudgy, wheezing man a head shorter than she was. An emissary from some country Holly had never heard of, he spoke immaculate English.

Following that, she was waltzed around the enormous room by a man wearing a bright-gold cummerbund and a dazzling array of medals. He was an ambassador from one of the Slavic countries.

When Howard and Maggie deigned to make their appearance, there was a hush and all eyes were upon them. Maggie looked every inch the first lady, and despite the unspoken strain between them, Holly was proud of her.

The president and first lady danced together then, the crowd moving back for them, the Secret Service agents looking on as alertly and unemotionally as ever, ready to pounce upon anyone foolish enough to make a wrong move.

Looking at David, Holly despaired. This was not the man who had loved her with such sweet ferocity the night before. This was a stranger, an automaton.

Some minutes later, Holly had her dance with the president of the United States, his last before retiring with Maggie from the festivities. "No glass slippers, I see," he teased as they waltzed, flashbulbs bursting all around.

Holly laughed. "No. I ordered a pair from Saks, but they didn't have my size."

Howard responded with a laugh of his own, but he looked tired. Holly thought of how the next four years would age him and felt sad.

"When you see your brother tomorrow morning, Holly, you tell him I'll do all I can to see he gets the help he needs."

"Thank you," Holly replied softly. "For both of us."

Howard nodded somberly. "I'm just sorry it had to come to this," he said. "You'll be with us a few more days, won't you?" he added a moment later, deliberately changing the subject.

Holly shook her head. "I've got to get home to my nephew and my work, I'm afraid. If I possibly can, I want to leave tomorrow, after I see Craig."

Howard responded politely, then the dance was over. A few minutes later he left the ballroom with Maggie and their Secret Service entourage, David included. Holly remained at the party for another half hour and then departed, leaving no glass slipper behind.

It was late and David was exhausted. Like several of the other agents assigned directly to the president, he had worn a tuxedo, and he was eager to hurl the thing into the depths of his closet and forget it existed.

Walt Zigman sat at his desk, as always, oblivious to the late hour. A widower, his children grown and gone, he had nothing better to do, David guessed. He hoped to God his own life would never come down to that.

He laid his identification card and the earphone down on the desk.

"You told me you'd stay until inauguration week was over!" Walt blustered, his jowls quivering, his cigar bobbing between his teeth.

"I lied. I'm out, Zigman. Gone."

Zigman swore. "I knew it. I damned knew it."

David sighed and stuffed his hands into the pockets of his trousers. "I suppose Ranford gave you a full report on last night," he said, his eyes linked with Walt's.

"We didn't get it on tape, if that's what you're talking about, Goddard. Tell me something, though. What is it about this Lewellyn woman that makes her different from all the others?"

David had a headache; he rubbed his temples with a thumb and forefinger. "If I knew that, Walt, I might be able to put two sane thoughts together."

"She feel the same way you do?" Walt was apparently in a fatherly mood. His eyes were averted, though, and he was cleaning his fingernails with an unbent paperclip.

David had been struggling with that question all day. It had distracted him, making it hard as hell to keep his mind on the president and the endless crowds at the swearing-in and at the ball he'd just left. Holly had certainly responded in bed the night before, but come the rueful morning, her aquamarine eyes had been full of doubts. Misgivings. And a grudge that just might last a lifetime.

"It will be a long time before she trusts me completely, if she ever does."

There was a short, reflective silence.

"I'm sorry about this whole thing, Goddard, for what it's worth. I should have sent someone else."

"You didn't know I was going to fall in love with Holly," David said, his jaw growing taut of its own accord and then relaxing again. "I didn't either."

Walt reached out and collected the earphone and the identification badge. "You keep in touch, Goddard. If things don't work out out there in Podunk, Washington, you come back here."

David had no answer for that. If things didn't work out in Spokane, he didn't know where he would go or what he would do. The only thing he could be certain of was that he was never going to come back to this job.

Leaving Walt's office, he squared his shoulders. Things would work out with Holly, dammit. He was going to *make* them work out.

## Chapter Twelve

Holly was delivered to Walter Reed Hospital first thing the next morning, as promised. She was, of course, flanked by the usual Secret Service set of two, but at least they stayed outside of Craig's room, exchanging toneless rhetoric with the FBI man who guarded the door.

Craig sat alone in the room, wearing a striped bathrobe that was too big for him, his gaze fixed on the panoramic view offered by a huge window.

Holly lifted her chin and gave herself a silent order not to cry. Her brother looked so broken, so small and in so much trouble. "Craig?"

He turned, his eyes sunken and circled. His face, stubbled with a new beard, looked gaunt; he might have been a hundred instead of just thirty-six. "Hello, Holly," he said, and his voice was as hollow as his eyes.

"Are they treating you well?" she asked, and the words sounded stiff, stilted. Talking to this wasted remnant of a man was not the same as talking to her brother.

Craig shuddered and executed a rueful parody of a smile. "They're not shining lights in my face and telling me they have ways of making me talk, if that's what you mean."

Holly had no plans to ask about the cocaine habit that had brought him to this pass; the ravages of his withdrawal, which would probably go on for some time, were clearly visible in his face.

She forced herself to go to him, to lay one hand on his thin shoulder. Touching him seemed to work some magic—he became Craig again. Tears stung in her eyes and ached in her throat as she bent to kiss the top of his head.

"Oh, Craig, how did this happen?"

His shoulder stiffened beneath her hand. "The way it always happens, Holly," he said brokenly. "You try cocaine and you're on top of the world. You can do no wrong. You're Superman, you're James Bond. And then one day you find out that you've gotta have the stuff and there aren't any choices anymore."

Holly swallowed hard and reached up with one hand to surreptitiously wipe away her tears. Her falling apart was not going to do Craig any good; she had to be strong now. "Is there anything I can do?" she whispered. "Special doctors, anything like that?"

Craig shook his head. "Forget I was ever born," he said hoarsely, looking at the view again. "That's the best thing you can do for yourself and for Toby."

There was nothing to say to that. If and when Craig overcame his cocaine problem, he might still be faced with a long prison term.

"You're still all tangled up with Goddard, aren't you?" Craig's question was so direct and so unexpected that Holly gaped at him for a moment, unable to answer. "He's bad news, Holly. For your own sake, walk away."

"That's going to hurt," she managed to say, at length.

Craig gave a humorless chuckle. "Lots of things hurt in this life, Holly. Too many things hurt. But Goddard used you and I don't want you to forget that. He'd use his own mother, if the Service asked him to. Believe me, I know."

Holly wound a finger in one of Craig's lank curls—once they had been so springy that she had teased him about them—and waited for him to go on.

"Find yourself a flesh-and-blood man, Holly," he complied after some time. "Goddard is a robot, like me. Like all the rest of them. He's nothing more than a hit man on the right side of the law."

Holly shivered. David wasn't a hit man! He wasn't!

"Lift your hand or a camera or a comb in the same room with the president or his lady sometime, Holly, if you don't believe me. You'll find yourself face-down on the floor with your hands cuffed before you catch your breath."

"There is a reason for that, Craig!"

He looked up at her. "Yes. But can you live with it, Holly? Can you live with guns and subterfuge and international intrigues that would curl your fingernails? Believe me, he knows things that he can't share with you, but they'll make him hell to live with all the same."

I love David, screamed some forlorn part of Holly's heart, I love him! "You needn't worry," she said aloud. "Anything that David and I might have had was over the moment I found out that it was you he wanted, not me."

They were silent again for a while, lost in their own thoughts, their own griefs and regrets.

"I'd better go," Holly said finally. "I've got a plane to catch."

"Right."

She came around to look into his face. "Is there anything I can send you, Craig? Books? Magazines? Anything?"

"Books," he said, and for a moment there was a hint of the old Craig, an inveterate reader, in his eyes. He even chuckled. "Nothing about spies, though, okay?"

Near tears again, Holly bent to kiss his forehead. "No spies," she promised, and then she hurried out lest she break down in front of him.

It was a relief to board the airplane, to leave the White House and the Secret Service and everything else behind. Everything except David.

Holly buckled her seat belt and pretended to listen as a flight attendant explained the mysteries of oxygen masks and No Smoking signs. She wondered if she should have called David and said good-bye. Said *something*.

Vigorously, she shook her head in answer to her own questions. It was better this way, better to make a clean break and forget all about Agent Goddard and his novel investigating techniques.

The plane was barreling down the runway; Holly closed her eyes and braced herself for the lurching leap it would take when it left the ground. She hated that part of flying, along with the full reverse thrust of the engines upon landing; it always made her feel as though the craft would go tumbling end over end.

A hand closed over her fingers, which were clutching the armrest with painful force. She opened her eyes just as the plane lunged into the air and the landing gear ground into place.

David. David was sitting in the seat beside hers, big as life.

Holly blinked her eyes, certain that she was hallucinating, but he was still there when she looked again. Wearing tan corduroy slacks, a brown cashmere turtleneck and a cocoa-colored leather jacket.

"It's me, all right," he said calmly.

"What are you doing here?"

He peeled her fingers from the armrest and soothed them between his own, lifting her hand and inspecting her nail polish with a slight frown, as though he didn't quite approve of the shade. "Take a wild guess," he said.

Holly finally gathered the presence of mind to wrench her hand free. "Just go and sit in some other part of the plane. Or better yet, why don't you jump out over Kansas?"

David chuckled and settled into the seat with a comfortable sigh. "I've never liked Kansas. Besides, we won't be there for a while yet. We're probably over Maryland."

"Maryland would do just as well, I'm sure," Holly snapped, turning her head and looking out over the wing and a floor of cumulus clouds trimmed in pink and gold.

"Give me until Kansas to win you over." There was a wry, injured sort of humor in David's tone.

She swung her eyes around, giving him a look that sliced deep. "Watch my lips," she said coldly. "We could fly to Hong Kong. We could fly to the moon. We could fly to *hell*, Mr. Goddard, and you couldn't win me over!"

The captain gave some garbled message over the speakers and the No Smoking and Fasten Seat Belt signs blinked out, making chiming sounds. The flight attendants reappeared with their smiles and their rattling service cart.

"You weren't even going to say good-bye?" David asked, and this time there was no hint of humor in his tone. He sounded hurt and more than a little bewildered.

For just a moment, Holly's impractical heart clogged her throat. She knew there were tears glistening in her eyes when she looked at him, but she couldn't help either the tears or the looking. "I didn't see any point," she managed to say.

His jaw tightened and he paled a little beneath his winter tan. Probably, Holly thought, it was a health-club tan, as artificial as the feelings he had claimed to have for her.

"I'm getting tired of playing the heavy. The investigation and Craig's arrest are both in the past; can't we go on from here?"

How Holly wished they could, but that would be asking too much. She might love this man—she *did* love this man with all her heart and all her soul—but what good was that without trust? And she was never, ever going to trust him.

"Maybe they're in the past for you," she said stiffly, shaking her head when a flight attendant stopped to offer liquid refreshments. After David had ordered and paid for a scotch and water, and the attendant had moved on, she finished, "I'm always going to remember, David. I'm going to remember your lies. I'm going to remember watching you handcuff my only brother in my kitchen."

"How about the way we made love, Holly? Are you going to remember that? Are you going to remember the things we said and did when our passion was so great that we couldn't bear it?"

Holly closed her eyes tight. "Don't!"

"Someone has to, Holly. What we had—what we have—is too rare and too precious to let go of without a fight. I've accepted that fact even if you haven't."

Holly snatched away his drink and took a gulp of it before handing it back, and David laughed.

"Face it, baby," he teased in an Edward G. Robinson voice, "you're stuck with a G-man!"

"I've already had to deal with all the 'G-men' I care to in this lifetime, thank you very much."

"We must be nearing Kansas. Do you still want me to jump?"

"More than anything," Holly sighed, unable to look at him now. If she did, she would tumble witlessly into those indigo eyes and the fall would be much deadlier than the one to Kansas. "What are you doing here, anyway? Don't you have to guard Howard or some visiting potentate?"

He hesitated and Holly sensed that he was hiding something—a possibility that infuriated her. "I've got some time off," he finally answered.

"I hope you're not going to Spokane," she replied in all honesty.

"I'm going wherever you go."

Holly sighed, sinking back into her seat. But when a flight attendant came by, she sat up straight again and announced in a clear voice, "Miss, this man is bothering me."

David laughed and the flight attendant looked him over in appreciative confusion, obviously wondering how a man like that could "bother" any woman in the unpleasant sense of the word.

"Is...is this true, sir?" asked the pretty attendant, not certain what to do.

"Oh, it's true all right," David confessed benevolently, rising from his seat and stepping into the aisle. He handed what remained of his drink to the stewardess and braced his hands against the back of the seat and the one just ahead. "And I'll go right on bothering you, Holly Llewellyn, because I love you. Because I need you."

Holly flushed with furious frustration and a need that rivaled the one he professed to feel. "You go to hell, Mr. Goddard," she replied, and then she fixed her eyes on the back of the seat in front of her and stared at the grubby tweed until it began to shift and undulate. When she dared to look, David was gone.

Holly felt a bereft sort of triumph. He meant to haunt her, he'd as much as said that straight out. He meant to follow her and pursue her until she gave in to him. And Holly was afraid she might do just that.

The airplane landed in Denver, where Holly was to catch her connecting flight to Spokane. Even before she looked back to confirm her suspicions, she knew that David was following her, she could feel him there, like a spectre.

She visited the rest room and the gift shop, trying to kill the hour layover, becoming more and more tense with every passing moment. Finally Holly whirled on David and hissed, "This is harassment! Leave me alone!"

He stepped closer, oblivious to the stream of people flowing around them on all sides, his eyes gentle. "Tell me you don't love me, Holly," he said quietly. "If you can truthfully say that, I'll go away."

Holly swallowed. That wasn't so hard, was it? Four little words, only four. I don't love you. She tried to say them and they would not pass her throat.

David waited patiently.

Holly tried again, failed again and turned away with a stifled sob, one hand to her face. David took her elbow in a firm grasp and escorted her into the nearest lounge. There, he settled her at a shadowy corner table, holding both her hands in his. At his request, a waitress in jeans and a western shirt brought two cups of coffee.

Holly freed one hand to lift her cup to her lips; some of the steaming brew inside sloshed over to burn her hand and stain the tablecloth. David deftly removed the cup and set it aside to cool.

"I want one chance with you, Holly. Just one chance. Can you give me that?"

"Wh-what if I say no?"

"Then I'll get on the next plane to Washington."

"What about that speech you made on the airplane? What about the way you've been following me ever since we landed?"

David sighed raggedly and looked away for a moment. "I'm sorry. The last thing you need is pressure, I know that. But I was desperate."

"Why?" Holly whispered, and the word sounded pained.

"Because I love you—as, I believe, I have already mentioned on several occasions."

Holly was weary, her head full of dizzying, unrelented images—herself, dancing with the president; Craig, looking so lost and broken; David, carrying her to his water bed, making love to her in a way that could still heat her blood. "I'm so confused," she muttered.

He squeezed her hand. "I know," he said softly. "Let me prove to you that I really do care, Holly. That's all I'm asking."

"How do you propose to do that, David?" Holly asked with a desperation that was more revealing than she could ever have guessed. "You'll always be the man who arrested Craig, the man who lied—"

"I'll always be the man who loves you," he reminded her.

And the man who carried Toby through a frightening crowd of reporters the day after Craig was arrested, Holly thought with disjointed hope. The man who set up the Christmas tree, the man who went out for chicken, the man who was hopelessly inept at flying model airplanes....

She gave herself a mental shake. "I don't think—"

"We'll date, that's all. We'll talk, get to know each other. And this time, it will all be on the level, Holly."

Her coffee had cooled; she took a steadying sip. Maybe David was right. Maybe there was a chance, if they could just approach the situation rationally and take their time. "No lovemaking," she ventured. "We have to start all over again, from square one. Agreed?"

David sighed. "Agreed," he replied with comic reluctance.

Their flight number was called and they left the table, David pausing to pay the check. Holly was settled into her seat on the airplane, pretending to read a magazine, when he caught up with her.

"Very cute," he muttered wryly, falling into his seat on the aisle.

Holly peered at him over the rims of her reading glasses, which she was certain he had never seen before. "Have we been introduced?" she asked primly.

David laughed and rolled his eyes.

The condominium David selected as his new home was in a round building, three floors from the top, and every outer wall was a window. The view was phenomenal, including Riverfront Park, the Spokane river itself and the old brick railroad tower. Division Street was a double strand of diamonds glimmering in the first shadows of twilight.

He sat down on the lushly carpeted floor, drew his knees up and wondered whether he was doing the right thing, uprooting himself like this. Maybe he hadn't liked his job, per se, but he was going to miss the excitement of living in Washington. He was going to miss Chris and his nieces. And his friends.

He stood up again, taking in the spacious, as-yet-unfurnished living room. Holly was here; that was the important thing. Chris and the girls could visit as soon as school let out. And he would make new friends.

The telephone sat on the floor, looking forlorn in the empty vastness of the room. David moved toward it, then held himself back. He'd promised to go slowly with Holly, promised not to pressure her. And he had to abide by those promises.

He went into the kitchen and opened the refrigerator, which contained a quart of buttermilk and a red-and-white bucket with one chicken wing in the bottom. David gnawed at that as he wandered from one elegant room to another, pondering the lengths he'd gone to just to be near Holly and regretting none of them.

The telephone rang, echoing in the emptiness, and David ambled toward the nearest one, expecting to hear from the real-estate agency or maybe the law school, where he was registered for review classes.

"David?" The familiar shrill of that voice almost made him choke on the chicken he'd been munching. "God, if you knew what I've been through, trying to track you down! I practically had to bribe Chris—"

"Marleen," David said woodenly. "Marleen?"

"I'm on leave," she chimed in bright response, as though she had never walked out when he'd needed her. As though she had never torn his guts out and stomped on them.

"What does that have to do with me?" he managed to ask, hoping that he didn't sound as hollow as he felt.

"We were married!" she sang. "Doesn't that entitle me to call up and say hello, David?"

"I find it hard to believe that you called just to say hello. What do you want? Money?"

There was a silence. "David!" Marleen wailed in injured good humor. "What an awful thing to say! We loved each other once."

"How are your monkeys?"

"Well, if you're going to be that way—"

David closed his eyes and the old pain was a sickness within him. He wished that Holly were there. "Wait," he said. "I was just surprised, that's all."

"Good." Marleen sounded pleased and perhaps a little relieved, which worried David. "Listen, sweetheart, I'm in L.A. right now, visiting the folks and all that." She paused, lowering her voice, presumably so the "folks" wouldn't overhear. "It's just a deadly bore, David, so I was wondering, well, since Spokane is a fairly short flight from here—"

"No," David broke in.

"No?"

David sat down on the floor, his head throbbing. He tossed the denuded chicken wing, because if he hadn't, he'd have tossed the telephone instead. "I mean, I'm just getting settled in here. And I'm flying back to Washington to sublet my place there and make arrangements for my furniture to be shipped. I really don't have time—"

"David, I was your wife!"

"You were the greatest single mistake of my life, Marleen," he said, thinking aloud.

He could almost see her pouting, see the tears welling in her enormous brown eyes.

"I guess I should have known I was going to get this kind of reception," she said. "Chris was positively cold when I called her."

David's head was pounding. "Look, Marleen, if you want money for some research project, apply for a grant. I really don't want to talk to you. And I sure as hell don't want to see you."

She sounded coy now, and just a little predatory. "Maybe you're scared, David. Scared that I might make you care again."

"If that's what you have in mind, don't waste your time. I'm in love with somebody else."

The moment that last sentence was out of his mouth, David knew it had been a terrible mistake. Marleen enjoyed a challenge, and saying that had been as good as flinging down a glove.

Having said too damned much already, David calmly and abruptly hung up the telephone. It rang again moments later; he lifted the receiver and dropped it into place.

The next morning, at twenty-five minutes after seven, he crawled, grumbling, out of the sleeping bag he had spread out in his future bedroom. The door bell buzzed repeatedly as he groped into his jeans and stumbled, cursing under his breath, to open the door.

Marleen stood in the hallway, her big teeth bared in a smile that brought the jungles of Borneo to mind, her light-brown, chin-length hair artfully rumpled.

"Mountain," she said, "meet Mohammed."

David groaned and rubbed his eyes. Maybe this was a bad dream. Maybe he was hallucinating.

"Aren't you going to ask me in?" Marleen wanted to know. "I could really use a cup of coffee and a hot shower."

"There are hotels all over town," David said, barring her way. "Check into one."

"I don't have the money to do that. I spent it all to fly home from Borneo and then come up here."

David cursed, making no effort to keep his voice down, but Marleen only laughed and shouldered her way past him, a suitcase in each hand, her eyes sweeping the empty condominium.

"I'll pay for your hotel," he offered lamely. It was too late and he knew it; short of throwing Marleen out bodily, which he considered doing, his choices were limited.

"Oh, David, stop being so tiresome. I'm not here to cause you any trouble."

"Then why?"

"For old time's sake, that's all. And maybe for a slight—" she winced appealingly "—contribution."

"Anything for your monkeys, Marleen," David said with biting grandeur, his arms sweeping out from his sides.

"Stop calling them 'monkeys,'" came the controlled response. "They're chimpanzees and they are an important link to the past."

"Are they? As far as I'm concerned, they're small, noisy, furry beasts that pick bugs off each other's hides for a snack."

Marleen set down her suitcases, her eyes flashing even though she was still smiling determinedly. "I didn't expect you to be so bitter after all this time, David. I really didn't."

"Bitter? Me?" David retorted acidly. "Why would I be bitter, Marleen? Why the goddamned hell would I be *bitter*?"

She subsided a little, her chocolate-colored eyes wide and suspiciously moist. "I'm sorry that I hurt you."

"Oh, thank you. That makes everything all right. I can feel my ulcers and residual neuroses healing right now!"

Marleen sat down on one of her battered suitcases, a forlorn, elfin creature in a rumpled raincoat, her face in her hands. "Oh, David, don't do this to me," she whispered. "Please—"

David stormed away from her into his bedroom. He'd packed for the flight to Washington the day before, and he was going to leave early. Pale with rage, he showered, then dressed in slacks, a white sweater and a sports jacket.

When he reached the living room, his own suitcase in hand, the hopes he'd had that Marleen would just go away went up in smoke. Her baggage was still sitting there, and he could hear her humming in the kitchen, the sound blending in with the chortling of the coffeepot.

"Damn," he rasped, wondering what to do, how to get Marleen out of his house, out of his life. The answer was a four-figure drop in his bank balance; he wrote out a check with violent strokes of his pen, laid the payoff beneath the handle of one of her suitcases and walked out, slamming the door behind him.

Downstairs, he got into one of the cabs that were almost always on hand, muttering to himself. He would be gone for a couple of weeks, he supposed, making arrangements for his furniture to be moved, saying various good-byes, giving away several hundred tropical fish.

Surely, by the time he'd driven his car across country—he needed the distance and monotony of the task to think—Marleen would have gone back to Borneo and her monkeys.

## Chapter Thirteen

The circular building towered over Riverfront Park. Holding Toby's model Cessna in both hands, Holly gazed up at it.

"Are we going to visit David?" Toby demanded eagerly, tugging at the sleeve of her pink windbreaker. "Are we, Mom?"

The bright, springlike shine of that late January day caused a painful catch in Holly's heart, as did Toby's question. It had been a full week since she and David had parted at the airport, agreeing to start over again. He had called just once in that time, and that had only been to pass on his new telephone number and address; he hadn't suggested they get together. Holly's feelings about that were mixed.

Toby tugged at her sleeve again, more forcefully this time. "Mom?" he prompted. "Couldn't we? Please?"

She looked down at the little boy and smiled. "Okay. We'll ask if he wants to come down here and fly the plane with us."

"And ride the carousel!" Toby beamed. "Don't forget, you promised that we could ride the carousel!"

They walked across the rolling, snow-patched lawns of the park, Toby straining to rush ahead, Holly holding back a little, wondering if it was wise to approach David. After all, they had an agreement, and she still had contradictory feelings toward him, stemming from the way they'd met.

"Toby, maybe we shouldn't..." she hesitated when they reached the main door of the exclusive building. There was a doorman on duty, perhaps he wouldn't even let them pass.

"Come on, Mom," Toby insisted, dragging her up to the entrance.

As the doorman looked her over, Holly was painfully conscious of her battered blue jeans, her T-shirt and windbreaker, her breeze-tumbled hair.

"May I help you?" asked the sentinel, his deep, rumbling voice ringing with genteel authority.

"My name is Holly Llewellyn and this is—"

The doorman's round face broke into a smile. "Go right up, Ms. Llewellyn. I can't say whether or not Mr. Goddard is at home, but I have orders to admit you at any time."

Holly was relieved; inwardly, she realized, she had been expecting to be turned away. Things were shaky between her and David, and there was always the possibility that he had decided their relationship wasn't worth the trouble.

She and Toby crossed the sumptuous, plant-filled lobby. There were two sets of elevators.

"What floor does David live on?" Toby queried when they were inside one of the elevators, his hand poised to punch the proper button.

"Seven," Holly answered immediately, then bit her lower lip. Her eagerness was showing, and she had to get it under control, letting David Goddard see how easily he could sway her would be foolish.

They arrived on the seventh floor in a whisk and stepped out into a spacious entryway, decorated, like the lobby, with plants.

David's condominium apparently took up the entire floor, for there was only one door in sight. Holly's hand trembled a little as she reached out to ring the bell. She drew a deep breath and summoned up a brave smile just as the door swung open.

A lovely woman wearing a colorful, tropical-print robe answered the door. "Yes?"

Holly was speechless, her imagination running away from her. Toby, on the other hand, had the presence of mind to ask ingenuously, "Is this where David Goddard lives?"

Wide brown eyes swept over Holly's Saturday-in-the-park clothes. "Yes, it is. I'm afraid David isn't home right now, though."

Holly, having surrendered the airplane to Toby, wedged her hands into the pockets of her windbreaker. A woman—good God, *a woman*—she tried not to panic or to jump to conclusions, but her emotions were so raw where David was concerned that she had almost no control over them. "Are you his sister?" she dared to ask.

The woman laughed, running one hand through her soft brown hair. "Good heavens, no. I'm his wife."

"His wife?" Toby echoed, confused.

Holly was outwardly calm. She squared her shoulders, caught Toby's free hand in her own and turned back toward the elevator. Over one shoulder, she said, "I'm sorry we bothered you."

"No problem," Mrs. David Goddard responded lightly, with a shrug of her silk-clad shoulders. "Shall I tell David you were here?"

Holly debated with herself for a moment, gnawing at her lower lip. "No," she said finally. "Don't tell him anything."

The concern in Toby's upturned face wrenched at Holly's heart. He was too young to understand this sort of betrayal, and she wondered how she would explain it all to him.

"I didn't get your names!" sang out the remarkably calm wife of the man Holly loved as the doors were closing.

"Toby and Holly!" the little boy shouted just before the doors swept shut.

Holly let go of her nephew's hand and sagged against the elevator wall, her hands gripping the polished brass railing, her eyes squeezed closed against tears of rage and hurt.

"What's-a-matter, Mom?" Toby wanted to know.

Holly dragged in a steadying breath and lifted her chin. "Nothing, Tobe. Nothing at all. Let's go back to the park and fly your plane, okay?"

"Okay," Toby agreed somewhat sadly. "But I wanted David to be with us."

"So did I," Holly replied with despairing dignity. "But sometimes things just don't turn out the way we hope they will."

Somehow, Holly got through the rest of that day, watching Toby's plane buzz in wide circles against a hurtfully blue sky, riding the fabled antique carousel, even choking down a hot dog. It was much later, when Toby had reluctantly taken his bath and tumbled into bed, that she sank into the chair at her desk in the kitchen, lowered her head to her arms and wept.

Being fooled once was bad enough; being fooled twice was devastating. Holly vowed that this was the last time, the very last time, that she would ever cry over David Goddard and his lies.

The trip across country had been a grueling one, and David was tired as he unlocked the door of his new condominium. He asked only one thing of the mysterious forces guiding the lives of mere mortals: that Marleen's failure to answer his telephone for the last week and a half meant that she was gone.

The movers had arrived ahead of him, and the furniture and crates they'd delivered looked ghostly in the dim light straying in through the open drapes. He paused a moment before flipping on the lights.

"Marleen?"

No answer. David shrugged out of his rumpled overcoat and flung aside the one suitcase he'd bothered to take with him. *There is a God,* he thought.

He checked the bedroom, which was full of boxes containing clothes and books, bed linens and towels. The water bed had been set up and filled, and he was grateful for that—now he wouldn't have to sleep on the floor or the couch.

"Marleen?" he ventured again. And that was when he saw the note affixed to the headboard of his bed with a piece of tape.

He snatched it into one hand, a peculiar sort of dread niggling in the pit of his stomach. "Darling,"

Marleen had written in a hand that resembled the efforts of one of her beloved apes. "I've gone back to my work. Thanks for the check and your backhanded hospitality. By the way, Holly came by. Is she your new love? I think she was surprised to find me here, and she said not to tell you that she stopped in. Ciao, Marleen."

David crumpled the note into a ball and flung it away on the strength of a growled curse. What Holly must have thought, encountering Marleen, of all people, was all too obvious.

He picked up the trail of the phone cord and followed it until he found the telephone beneath a pile of rumpled bath towels. Marleen had always been a slob. Holly's number leaped to his mind, but his finger hesitated over the buttons. It was late and this debacle called for more delicate handling than a midnight telephone call. Flowers, at the least, and some very fast talking.

David stiffened as he drew his hand back from the telephone. Dammit, why was he ready to grovel and beg when he hadn't done anything wrong? Whatever impression Marleen might have given—and he suspected that she had played the moment for every possible ounce of drama—the fact remained that he wasn't involved with her and hadn't been in years. Holly was a rational person and she would understand. She had to understand.

Too exhausted to think about the situation further, David staggered into the bathroom and took a long, hot shower, before making his way back to the bed. Marleen hadn't bothered to make it up again before she left, but he didn't care. He flung back the comforter and collapsed, falling asleep within seconds.

The next day was Saturday, and he awakened late. Standing at the windowed wall of his kitchen, he looked out over Riverfront Park, a cup of coffee in his hand, pondering the best way to approach Holly.

The weather was cold and sunny and there were a number of inveterate outdoor people in the park. He could see the carousel turning, a colorful blur inside its glass walls, and the sight uplifted him.

Momentarily, his eyes were drawn back to a small figure dashing in mad circles on the grass. David squinted and bent forward, trying to see. He couldn't so he opened a sliding door and went out onto the balcony surrounding his condo on all sides, resting his arms against the wrought-iron railing.

With the small person was a slightly larger one. One with golden-honey hair that shimmered in the sunshine of a false spring.

David grinned, went back inside, shutting the door behind him, and set his coffee cup aside with a resolute thump. He rummaged through boxes in the recreation room until he found his own model airplane, then put on a dark-blue windbreaker and went out.

He sprinted across the park until he was close enough to hear the buzz of Toby's plane, close enough to see them both. Toby was watching, his face upturned and bright with delight, while Holly skillfully executed swoops and dips and sharp turns with the radio-controlled toy.

Holly became aware of his presence by some sixth sense and turned to confirm the dizzying fact with her eyes. David was standing not twenty yards away, holding his airplane in his hands, watching her and Toby.

He looked fantastic in his jeans, navy-blue velour pullover and windbreaker, but Holly wasn't going to let things like that sidetrack her. Not this time. Gritting her teeth, she worked the handset, guiding her airplane in his direction in a wide sweep. "Bombs away," she whispered with evil relish as she plunged the lilliputian craft into a dive directed straight at his head. "Mom!" Toby bellowed, appalled.

David crouched, just barely escaping the airplane; it buzzed into another turn and came back toward him.

"Mom, don't!" Toby shrieked. "Don't! You'll hurt him."

"I want to hurt him," Holly replied grimly as David fell facedown in the snow-laced ground to avoid having a miniature Cessna embedded in his back. "Oh, boy, do I want to hurt him."

"Will you stop it!" David roared. Holly noted with satisfaction that the man had no sense of humor. "You're going to kill me!"

Holly brought the plane down again, letting it pass within inches of David's head. Toby, his face flushed with righteous indignation—he'd had lecture after lecture on how to operate that airplane safely—wrenched the controls out of her hands and guided the plane in for a smooth landing.

David sprang to his feet, his eyes snapping, a white line of annoyance edging his jaw. "If you're not happy to see me," he hissed, "just say so!"

Toby was looking frantically from one adult to the other, tears shimmering in his eyes, the handset shaking in his hands. "That was a crazy thing to do, Mom!" he shouted.

Looking down at him, Holly softened.

"You're damned right it was!" yelled David.

Holly shifted her gaze from Toby to David, piercing him with it. And then she turned on her heel and stomped away, toward the carousel, Toby scrambling along beside her like a puppy.

David halted her progress from behind, catching her elbow in his grasp and handing his airplane to Toby in one simultaneous motion. "If this wasn't a public place, lady, I would turn you over my knee," he said through his teeth.

Holly wrenched her arm free. "Stay away from me, you creep!"

*"Mom!"* Toby wailed, mortified.

She plunged one hand into the pocket of her jacket, pulling out a string of tickets. "Here!" she said to her nephew, with uncommon impatience. "Go and ride the carousel!"

Toby looked uncertain, his china-blue eyes again darting from Holly's face to David's.

"Go ahead, slugger," David urged in a gruff undertone, taking both toy planes from the little boy's arms. "Everything is going to be all right."

After one more glance at Holly, one so wary and concerned that it made her wince inwardly, Toby bounded off to enter the round building housing the carousel. The music of the calliope seemed ludicrous, in light of the situation.

His jaw still working with suppressed outrage, David set the planes aside on the grass and lifted his hands to his hips, watching Holly, his gaze burning into her face and finally forcing her to lift furious, tear-blurred eyes.

"What did Marleen tell you?" he asked when he had her full attention.

Holly shrugged, though she was on the verge of flinging herself at David Goddard kicking and scratching and hissing like a she-cat. Her whole body quivered with the need to attack, to hurt. "Only that she is your wife," she said, marveling at the calmness of her voice. She had expected the words to come out as a shriek.

"And you immediately decided that I had lied to you again," David muttered. Damn him, he didn't look the least bit apologetic; instead, he appeared angry enough to forget that this was a public place and make good on the threat he had issued earlier.

Some of Holly's indignation faded away, driving a slow, pink blush up over her cheeks. "When presented with the evidence, I naturally—"

"You naturally found me guilty!"

Holly retreated a step. "She said—"

"I can imagine what she said! The truth is that we've been divorced for years, just like I told you before!"

People were beginning to stare and the calliope music went merrily on. Holly was getting a headache. "She had on a bathrobe. She was in your apartment—"

"And I was on my way to Washington," David broke in again, more calmly this time, though his tone was sliced deep.

Holly was about to start believing him again and she'd sworn she would never do that. She whirled away, stomped into the carousel building and bought herself a ticket. When the ride stopped, she climbed onto a ferocious looking tiger, spotting Toby ahead on a white horse.

The carousel began to turn, going faster and faster. Holly was dizzy and ill all of a sudden, and she clasped the pole in front of her with both hands. When she opened her squeezed-shut eyes, David was perched, sidesaddle, on the black panther beside her, his chin propped in his hands.

Holly held on tighter, feeling the color drain from her face. "I don't think I...feel very well..." she managed to say.

David's face gentled, his eyes scanning her face. She could barely hear him over the thrill piping of the calliope. "Do you want me to tell them to stop this thing?"

Holly shook her head, then rested it against the pole she was still holding with a death grip. What was wrong with her? She had ridden this carousel a thousand and one times. Though it moved rapidly, it was not the sort of ride that could bring her breakfast burning up into her throat.

Finally, mercifully, the carousel stopped turning. Holly was trembling as David pried her hands loose from the pole and lifted her down. She might have stumbled, but he held her firmly, prepared to lift her into his arms and carry her, if necessary. She didn't dare let that happen.

Outside, she drew in fresh air in greedy gasps, praying that she wouldn't disgrace Toby by throwing up in public.

David ushered her to a brightly painted bench, sat her down and went off, returning within moments with a glass of water from a concession wagon several yards away.

"What's wrong?" he asked, bracing one foot against the bench and watching her as she sipped the water, his arms folded across his chest.

"I don't...know," Holly confessed quite honestly. "I must have the flu or something."

"Or something," David muttered, and he sounded so wistful that Holly's eyes shot to his face.

Toby, evidently worried about Holly, had gotten off the carousel and gone to fetch the airplanes and their handsets. He stood a little way apart, watching with large, saucerlike eyes.

"Are you sick again, Mom?" he asked.

"Again?" David demanded, leaning forward slightly.

Toby came a few steps closer, still a bit wary of these two strange adults. "Mom's been getting sick a lot lately. I want her to go to the doctor."

"So do I," David said quietly. "Can you walk now, Holly, or shall I carry you?"

Holly stood up determinedly and nearly sank to the bench again, she was so dizzy. Her stomach was doing leaps inside her. How on earth was she going to drive home in this condition?

David smiled reassuringly at Toby, ruffling his hair, and then casually lifted Holly off her feet, holding her against his chest like a child. She was too queasy to resist.

"My car is...over there..." she offered.

"You're in no shape to drive," David said flatly, looking down at Toby. "Can you manage the planes, slugger?"

Toby swelled with confidence, reassured by David's calm manner. "Sure I can. Can you manage Mom?"

David threw back his head and laughed and Holly was soothed by the scent of his hair and skin, and by the strength of him. "I don't think anybody can manage your mom," he answered presently, "but I mean to try."

"Put me down," Holly said.

"No way," came the implacable answer. "You're going to my place and you'll take it easy until you feel better."

"I can walk!"

"I know, but I like carrying you."

"David, you are making a scene! Now, put me down this minute!"

David was striding off toward the condominiums, his hold on Holly as firm as ever. "You know something, woman?" he teased, his breath whispering through her hair. "You're getting completely out of line here. You need someone to take a firm hand—"

Holly stiffened again and made a strangled sound of furious protest. "I don't need anything of the sort!" she blustered. "I'm a grown woman, perfectly capable—"

David lowered his voice, even though Toby was already bounding ahead, out of earshot, eager to see the place where his hero lived. "We both know what you need, don't we?"

The queasiness had passed and Holly was not only able to walk on her own, she was desperate for it. "Damn you, David," she hissed in a scathing undertone, "you promised!"

He sighed and set her on her feet. "So I did," he said. Knowing that she wasn't going to bolt without Toby, he slowed his strides to stay in step with her. "Holly, could you be pregnant?"

Pregnant! Holly simmered, clenching her fists at her sides. This man was just full of heartening suggestions! But as she walked, she did some mental counting and subsequently felt the warmth seeping out of her face to pool in a hot puddle in the pit of her stomch.

"Oh, my God," she moaned, stopping cold.

David caught her arm and pulled her into motion again, propeling her into the building, through the lobby and into the elevator Toby was holding for them. Soon enough, they were inside David's lush, if cluttered, digs.

"I didn't think spies made this much money," Toby observed with the innocence of someone about to turn eight.

David and Holly both laughed. For Holly, it was involuntary. David, on the other hand, seemed relaxed, even happy.

He pressed Holly into a seat on the navy blue sofa she remembered from his apartment in Washington, D.C. and then abandoned her to take Toby on a guided tour of the new place.

"Pardon me," Holly wanted to call out after him, "but I think I'm pregnant here. Aren't we even going to discuss it?"

She sank back against the sofa cushions, her heart in her throat, one tear slipping down her cheek. You chickens, Holly Llewellyn, she thought with a bittersweet sort of joy, have just come home to roost. You danced and now you're going to have to pay the piper. Your jig is up.

Having run through all her favorite clichés, Holly wiped away the tear and sniffled, then sat up very straight.

"Stay off the balcony," she heard David telling Toby, in another room. "And don't fill up the hot tub."

"Right," Toby sang, eager to be obedient. Not for the first time, Holly resented his desire to please David; it wasn't an emotion she was proud of, but she seized it to keep from thinking about the baby that might, even now, be growing inside her. David's baby.

David came to her and sat down on the sofa beside her, drawing one booted foot up to rest on the opposite knee. "We can talk about this now," he said reasonably, "or we can wait until Toby isn't around. The choice is yours."

Holly swallowed hard. "Are all the choices mine?" she ventured softly.

David met her eyes directly. "Actually, no. If you are pregnant, the child is mine, too."

A least he didn't question that. Holly sighed and knotted her hands together in her lap.

He pried one free and held it tightly. "I'm sorry, Holly," he said in a voice so low that Holly had to strain to hear him. "I wanted you so badly that I didn't stop to ask if you were protected."

Again Holly sighed. She couldn't help being struck by his willingness to take responsibility so readily. "I wasn't taking the pill. I...I wasn't sleeping with anyone and—"

"It's all right, Holly."

"It isn't all right!" she argued sharply. Then, regretting her outburst, she struggled to take control of her emotions again, to lower her voice. "I'm single, David! And as much as I love Toby, raising him alone isn't easy! How will I manage two children?"

His thumb stroked the length of her fingers. "You would have the baby, then?"

She stared at him, her eyes wide. "Of course I would," she whispered.

"Thank God," he muttered, looking away again. Holly saw a touching struggle for composure going on in his face and loved him desperately for it.

"I'm scared, David," Holly confessed after a long, painful silence.

He pulled her close and held her against the hard curve of his shoulder. "Me, too," he said hoarsely. "Me, too."

The marriage proposal that Holly both hoped for and dreaded was evidently not forthcoming. David got up off the couch as Toby came in, blurting out, "Geez, David, your place in fantastic!"

I would have had to say no anyway, Holly said to herself, searching for comfort within. It's a good thing he didn't ask me again. It's a good thing.

But if it was such a good thing, another part of Holly wondered, why was it that she had to turn her face away to hide a new crop of despairing tears?

I can't panic here, David thought as he pulled a plate of cold pizza from the refrigerator and slid it into the microwave oven. I've got to remain calm.

Toby sat at the table, looking up at him with trust and liking shining in his face. For the millionth time, David thought how much he would like to raise this kid, fly model airplanes with him and root for him at Little League ball games.

And the other child, the child that might be born—

He couldn't think about that child, he didn't dare. If it turned out that Holly wasn't pregnant after all, it was going to be the worst disappointment of his life. No, whatever he did, he had to keep his head and go slowly and patiently.

Patience, hell, David decided. He was going to walk into that living room, get down on his knees and beg Holly Llewellyn to marry him.

When he got there, she was gone. After a moment of alarm, he heard her in the bathroom, throwing up.

And he had never loved her more.

## Chapter Fourteen

There was no way Holly could wait until Monday to find out whether or not she was going to have a baby, but she couldn't quite bring herself to put in an appearance at a hospital emergency room, either. Was there such a thing as an emergency pregnancy?

Holly's hands tightened on the steering wheel of the car. Beside her, the seat belt drawn across his small body, Toby slept peacefully. He'd fallen asleep at David's, and David had wanted them both to stay...

Holly pulled the car to a stop in front of an all-night drugstore and looked back at the huge cylindrical building towering against the night sky. The lights of David's condo burned like sweet beacons, pulling at her. God, how she'd wanted to stay. How she'd wanted to fall into David's arms, David's bed.

She let her forehead rest against the steering wheel. Even now, it was all she could do not to go back, carrying Toby in her arms as David had carried him down to her car, and ask if he might not have room in his life for two—perhaps two and a half—more people.

But Holly couldn't do that, of course. Not until she knew what she truly felt and what she truly wanted. A baby might be the world's oldest reason for getting married; it was also the world's worst. And besides, David had not mentioned marriage again.

Grimly, Holly got out of her car and locked it, then hurried into the drugstore. There, she bought a home pregnancy test.

At home, she awakened Toby and half ushered, half carried him inside. "We should have stayed at David's," he yawned out as he groped his way up the stairs.

"Right," Holly said, smiling even though she was ready to cry. The paper bag containing her pregnancy test rattled a little in her hand.

"He has a hot tub," Toby argued sleepily. "Right in his bedroom."

"That clinches it," Holly teased. "A man with a hot tub in his bedroom is a person to be reckoned with."

A hot tub in his bedroom, she reflected as she went into the kitchen to check the answering machine and have one last cup of coffee. Or was it to put off taking that drugstore test and finding out whether or not she really was pregnant?

She poured a cup of cold coffee and put it in the microwave to heat. There was one message on the machine, from Elaine, if it could be called a message. Her friend sounded cryptic and excited and hesitant, all at once, but she hadn't really said anything.

With a sigh, Holly took her coffee from the microwave, was instantly nauseated by the smell of it and poured it down the sink. Then, resolutely, she snatched up the innocuous little bag that seemed to contain her, Toby's and David's fate, and she marched up the stairs.

"The test was positive," Elaine echoed with a sigh, her hands clenched tight around her coffee cup. "Well, Holly, clue me in; is that awful news or are we talking balloons and noisemakers here?"

Throughout the long, lonely Sunday just past, Holly had agonized over that very question. And she hadn't been able to come up with a clear answer. "I feel panic-stricken," she confessed. "I also feel like shouting for joy."

"Have you told David?"

Holly had reached for the telphone a thousand times on Sunday, for her car keys a thousand more. But in the end, she had not been able to face David. She was too afraid of leaning on him, too afraid of needing him for the wrong reasons. And too afraid, when she could bring herself to face it, that he would either reject her outright or offer to marry her for the sake of the baby.

"No," she said finally.

"I won't give you the he-has-a-right-to-know speech, Holly," Elaine replied, her voice gentle. "I don't think you need that right now."

"I've given it to myself a hundred times." She paused and assessed her friend. "You have something to tell me, don't you?" she prompted, remembering the brief, disjointed message Elaine had left on the machine over the weekend.

Elaine's pretty face seemed a little drawn. "This is a lousy time to bring it up, but yes, I do have something to tell you. I've been offered a fantastic job, Holly—an editorial position with a regional magazine."

Holly knew what was coming then, and though she would hate losing Elaine, she couldn't help being happy for her. It was the kind of job her friend had always wanted, the kind of job she had been trained for. "That's wonderful, Elaine," she said softly.

Elaine's wide green eyes lifted to Holly's face. "You're not angry?"

"You were the best assistant anybody could have hoped to have, Elaine. But you've outgrown this job. It's time for a change."

"I'll stay until the new book is indexed," Elaine offered, and though she was smiling, there were tears shimmering in her eyes.

"No need. I can do that myself. You just go out there and set local publishing on its ear!"

Elaine laughed and sniffled, both at the same time. "To think I dreaded this so much. Poor Roy—I cried and fretted all weekend, I was so sure you would be upset. That offer couldn't have come at a worse time."

Holly sighed. "I'm not sure I agree, Elaine. The truth is, I think it might be time for my life to take on a new direction, too."

Elaine's eyes widened. "What are you saying, Holly?"

"I seem to be making the decision even as we talk, but thinking about it, I realize that I've wanted to make several changes for a very long time. I hate traveling so much, for one thing, having to leave Toby behind, and, well, cookbooks aren't much of a challenge anymore. I'd like to find out if I can write something different, Elaine. Something completely different.''

"Such as?" Elaine prodded with a genuine interest that touched Holly and gave her courage.

"Maybe a novel," she blurted out bravely.

"Wow!" Elaine beamed. "And I thought you were going to resign yourself to motherhood!"

"Motherhood is wonderful, Toby has already proven that beyond any shadow of a doubt. But I know I need something more. Is that terrible?"

"Of course it isn't terrible. But," Elaine paused, turning her coffee mug in an idle circle, "I'm still old-fashioned enough to think that kids need a father as well as a mother. Holly, are you going to marry David?"

An awkward silence fell. "You know that he gave me a ring at Christmas, I suppose," Holly ventured after a time.

Elaine all but smirked. "I guessed as much. After all, I was the one who hid his packages in the tree so you wouldn't fly mad and send them back in the next mail." She paused, then frowned, her eyes on Holly's left hand. "But I don't see a diamond."

"I gave it back," Holly confessed brokenly. "I was so angry with him, so hurt over that whole deception. And then Craig's arrest—"

"You've dealt with all that now?"

Holly sighed. "I thought I had. I love David so much, Elaine; I think I have from the first. And the more I saw him, the less those things seemed to matter."

"So what's the problem now?"

"There are several problems, actually. I don't know whether David even wants to marry me now. And I'm wondering how much of my—my caring for him is really caring and how much is panic at the idea of having a baby all by myself."

Elaine looked exasperated. "The solution is simple, Holly. You need time to think, time to get your head together, as the kids say. I mean, with all that's happened to you in the past few months, how can you expect to have a handle on everything?"

Holly tangled her fingers in her hair as if to pull it out by the roots. "Think! How can I think, Elaine? That man sends me into fits of confusion every time I see him."

"Then don't see him for a while," Elaine said flatly. "Call a time-out. Give yourself a chance to catch your breath."

"That might be easier said than done," Holly fretted, lifting her own coffee cup to her mouth. She felt her stomach leap at the smell and set the cup back down without taking a sip.

Her grimace made Elaine grin. "Everything is easier said than done," she agreed, patting Holly's hand. "But what the hell?"

"Yeah," Holly replied with a wry arch of one eyebrow. "What the hell?"

The two women spent the rest of that day determining what had to be done to wrap up Holly's lucrative career as a cookbook author. There was one more set of classes to teach at the department store and the manuscript on Chinese cooking had to be edited and then indexed. The newspaper column could be stopped with a month's notice.

Elaine had already gone home, taking a copy of the new manuscript with her, when the telephone rang. Holly drew a deep breath and answered it with a hello meant to sound cheerful. Except it came out a little hollow.

"Did you see your doctor?" David demanded without preamble, his voice gentle but gruff with weariness.

Holly closed her eyes a moment, stung by David's tone. He was hoping that she would say she wasn't pregnant, that he would be let off the hook. "Not yet," she said. "I have an appointment tomorrow morning."

"You're certainly casual about this, I'll say that for you!" David snapped. "I've been sweating blood ever since Saturday and you say you 'have an appointment tomorrow'!"

A tear slid down Holly's cheek. So much for never crying over David Goddard again. "I'm not being 'casual,' David, believe me," she managed to say. "I bought one of those home tests."

"And?"

"And—" Holly drew a deep breath to steady herself "—and it was positive."

There was a shattering silence at the other end of the line. "Are those things conclusive?" David finally asked, and there was no anger in his tone, but there was no happiness, either.

"I don't know," Holly admitted wearily. "I've never used one before."

"Very funny," came the ragged response.

"I wasn't joking, David."

He sighed; in her mind, Holly could see him leaning back in his chair, his thumb and forefinger to his temples. "I'd like to go with you tomorrow," he said finally, and still there was nothing in his voice to tell Holly what he was thinking.

She thought she knew that all too well. He was probably castigating himself for getting involved with a woman who didn't have enough sense to use birth control. "That won't be necessary, David," she said coldly, hanging up in his ear.

The telephone immediately rang again.

"Don't hang up on me, Holly," David warned. "I hate it."

Holly didn't hang up, but she did begin to cry, helplessly and with all the attendant noise. "Please, David...don't insist on going to the doctor's office with me...I couldn't bear it..."

"Holly." The word was a reprimand, but it was unbelievably gentle.

"I mean it, David!" Holly wailed. "I can't think clearly when you're around...I..."

He spoiled the intangible comfort he had just offered by swearing in a brutal undertone and then snapping, "Neither of us was thinking clearly from the beginning! Why start now, Holly?"

"David!"

"You should have stayed here the other night, Holly," he went on, quietly cruel. "What the hell? We could have made love until dawn. After all, the damage has been done!"

Damage. The word sliced through Holly like a knife. How could he call their baby, their precious child "damage"? "I hate you, David Goddard," she hissed into the receiver, keeping her voice down only because Toby might be near enough to hear. "Do you hear me? I hate you and I never want to see you again!"

The silence was charged. Holly braced herself for David's answer, but in the end, he gave none. There was a soft click and the line went dead.

In the morning, Holly kept her appointment with her doctor and was told for a certainty that she was pregnant. The baby would be born, she was blithely informed, in late September or early October.

Holly stumbled out of her doctor's office, vitamin prescriptions in hand, stricken by a combination of joy and despair. David was waiting beside the elevator doors.

"Well?" he asked simply, his voice hoarse. Holly was too distracted to even attempt to read the expression in his navy blue eyes. She nodded, her throat too thick to permit speech.

"When?" he prompted, not unkindly.

"Fall," she croaked.

The elevator arrived and David ushered Holly inside. But she didn't look at him, and as far as she could tell, he didn't look at her, either. How could this be? They had made this baby together, in passion so intense that Holly ached to remember it, and now they had nothing to say to each other. Nothing at all.

Out on the busy streets, people were rushing by, it seemed to Holly, in a colorful, threatening blur. Where had she left her car? Had she even brought the car?

No. She'd taken the bus. She remembered now. She had definitely taken the bus.

She tried in vain to recall which stop to wait at for another. Considering that she had lived in Spokane all her life and taken buses into virtually every part of it since the age of eleven, it was annoying to forget the routes and schedules now.

David's hand was strong on her elbow. "Come on," he said gruffly.

Holly looked at him with dazed, tear-blurred eyes. "Where are we going?"

"My place."

That snapped her out of it. She wrenched her arm free and went rigid. "Why, David? To do more 'damage'?"

Pain moved deep in his eyes, but was overcome so quickly that she thought she'd imagined it. "To talk," he said firmly, and his hand again closed around her arm.

"I don't want to talk to you, David. I don't want to talk to anybody. I just want to lie on my bed and cry."

The statement seemed to wound him; he looked away, scanning cloud-dappled blue skies for a moment. "All right," he said after a long time. "All right. But, please, let me get you a cab."

It seemed the least he could do, after fathering a baby he didn't want. "Thank you," Holly replied woodenly.

But when she reached her house, high on the South Hill, she did not lie down on her bed and cry. Elaine was there, working on the manuscript, and Madge was cleaning furiously. Both of them were trying so hard to be subtle that Holly forgot her misery for the time being and burst out laughing.

"Yes!" she yelled, spreading her hands wide of a body that would soon swell to pearlike proportions. "I'm pregnant!"

Faced with the certainty, her friends did not seem to know whether to celebrate or commiserate. Thinking it enough that she wasn't flying apart in pieces, Holly gave them no clue. She simply sat down at her desk and turned on her computer and began working on the last of the cooking columns she was required, by contract with the local newspaper, to write.

For the next two weeks, Holly lived in a frenetic kind of limbo, working day and night, praying that David wouldn't call or come by and leaping every time the telephone or door bell rang.

David didn't call, though. And he didn't come by. Holly was resigned to the fact that, despite his earlier claims to love and want her, she was going to have this baby alone. And raise it alone.

The fates seemed to respect her secret grief, however, and even to aid her in holding up the front she maintained for Elaine and Madge and Toby. Everything went well; Holly's agent accepted her decision to switch from sure-thing cookbooks to novels that might or might not sell, the newspaper was gracious, though they said their readers would miss her columns, and the department-store people didn't give her any flack, either, beyond reminding her that her contract called for one more set of lessons to be taught.

Yes, everything was fine. Until the night Toby ran away.


David was developing a hatred for coffee. He scowled at his empty cup and set it in the sink, looking out over the lights of the city and despairing. Why was he beating the books, night after night, like some college kid? For what?

He sighed raggedly and ran one hand through his hair. For his sanity, that was for what, he admitted to himself. If he didn't bury himself in classes by day and law books by night, he would go crazy. Perversely, he wondered what Holly was doing at that moment. What she was thinking and feeling.

Love for her clenched within David in a spasm so painful that it nearly bent him double. He had to leave her alone; he had to, no matter what the cost. A long talk with Holly's assistant, Elaine Bateman, had convinced him of that. And yet it was the hardest thing he had ever had to do—his every instinct ran counter to this endless, agonizing waiting.

The door bell rang and David's heart lunged to the pit of his stomach and then swelled into his throat. Let it be her, he thought desperately as he strode to the door and reached for the knob.

Forcibly, David stopped just short of opening it, drew a deep breath and tried to compose himself. It was crucial to say the right thing, to do the right thing— The bell rang again, insistently and David grinned as he turned the knob and pulled the door open.

Toby was standing before him, head down, jacket askew, his toy Cessna in one hand and the robot David had sent at Christmas in the other.

David scanned the hallway, puzzled, but saw no sign of Holly. Then, hiding the alarm he felt, he crouched to look into the little boy's averted face. It was tear-stained and pink from the cold outside.

Toby looked at him then and David ached at the despair he saw in that small face; it seemed to crumple before his very eyes.

"Don't you want to marry Mom and me?" the child wailed, flinging his arms around David's neck, the plane and the robot thumping to the floor.

David held him and rose to his feet, too overcome to respond immediately. After a time, though, he cleared his throat and asked, "Does your mom know where you are, slugger?"

The small head shook against his shoulder.

David had already guessed the answer to that question, of course, but it made an opening. "I think we'd better call her and tell her you're safe. Right now."

"Okay," sniffled Toby.

His shirt sodden with Toby's tears, David ruffled the little boy's hair and set him gently down on the sofa. This would be the first call he'd made to Holly in weeks, but his fingers didn't hesitate over the buttons as they usually did.

She answered, frantic, on the first ring. "Toby?"

"He's here with me," David said gently. "And he's all right."

"Thank God!" Holly wept. "Oh, thank God! I thought—"

David had to close his eyes for a moment. For some damned, inexplicable reason, he felt like crying himself. He didn't speak because he didn't dare.

"When did he get there?" Holly demanded, sniffling. "What did he say?"

The little boy's words echoed in David's heart. *"Don't you want to marry Mom and me?"*

"He hasn't said anything much," David lied gruffly, for Holly's sake as well as his own. "How the devil do you suppose he got all the way down here by himself?"

Holly sighed; David could see her in his mind, her wonderful aquamarine eyes puffy, her hair tangled from repeated, nervous ruffling. "I shudder to think," she said.

"Shall I bring him home or do you want to come and get him?" Either way, David despaired in silence, how am I going to be able to bear seeing you? Can that possibly be worse than *not* seeing you?

Holly's answer surprised him. "C-Could you keep him, just for tonight?"

David glanced back at Toby, who was watching him from the sofa, his lower lip jutting out in some kind of little-kid defiance. "Keep him?" he echoed, and Toby's eyes widened.

"Evidently it was important to him to see you, David. Maybe you can find out what made him do this."

"I'll try," David promised hoarsely, and then he said good-bye to Holly and turned back toward the child, folding his arms across his chest.

"Okay, slugger. What's the deal? How did you get down here alone?"

Toby was scrambling out of his jacket, ready to stay for the duration, but there was a challenge in his eyes. "Everybody thinks I'm too little to do anything," he complained. "Just like that dumb baby."

Bingo, thought David, but he didn't smile. He didn't want Toby to think that running away in the middle of the night was clever.

"What dumb baby is this?" he asked.

"The one Mom's going to have. She won't want me anymore, that's for sure."

"Oh? And on what do you base that conclusion, counselor?"

Toby squared his shoulders. At least he'd had supper before setting out on the crosstown journey—half of it was still on his striped T-shirt. "I'm not really hers, you know," he said.

"Mmmm."

"She's really my aunt."

"Right. You just call her 'Mom' to make her feel good, huh?"

Toby considered and seemed to find the idea magnanimous enough to claim. "Yeah."

"She loves you, Toby. And no matter how many babies she has, that is never going to change."

The uncertainty in Toby's face was painful to see. "You really think so?"

"I really think so. Now, how did you get here?"

"You won't belive it."

"Indulge me," David replied.

"I walked."

"All the way from the South Hill?" David was horrified, though he did a creditable job of hiding it.

"All the way from the South Hill," Toby confirmed proudly. But his grin faded away. "If Mom loves me so much, how come she said you could keep me?"

"She just meant for tonight, slugger. She's a smart lady—she figured that if you wanted to see me badly enough to run away, well, then she should let you see me."

"Oh. Are you going to marry us? Mom and me and the baby?"

David reeled inwardly but again managed to recover. "I'd like that a lot, Toby, but sometimes things don't go the way we want them to, no matter how hard we try. And right now, you'd better be thankful that I'm *not* married to your mom."

"Why?" demanded Toby, a study in disbelief.

"Because I'd give you the worst spanking you've ever had in your whole life, that's why. Running away is an ultra-dumb thing to do."

Toby pondered this carefully, his face working as he weighed getting spanked against having David for a father. "I guess the KGB could have got me," he said after due consideration.

"What do you know about the KGB?"

"I know they were after my dad."

David went to the sofa and sat down beside Toby, making a big deal of stretching his legs and crossing his booted feet on the glass top of the coffee table. "They're not going to bother you, Tobe," he said after a long time.

Toby looked relieved. "Good. I thought they might think my dad told me a secret or something."

David put one arm around the little boy and held him close. He could understand the depths of Holly's feelings for this child, for he already loved Toby as if he were his own.

"Would you really have spanked me if I'd been your kid?" Toby asked when the silence grew too long for comfort.

"You'd better believe it," David replied honestly. "There are certain things a guy just doesn't do, and running away is one of them."

Blue eyes the size of Frisbies looked up into David's face. "I think I'd still like to be your kid anyway," he said.

David laughed because if he hadn't, he'd have cried.

"You'll probably like the baby better'n me, just like Mom."

"Neither of us will like the baby better than you, Toby."

Toby snuggled close, beneath David's arm. "Babies can't fly Cessnas or nothin'," he said derisively. And then he fell asleep.

David removed Toby's shoes, slipped a pillow beneath his head and covered him with a down-filled quilt from one of the extra bedrooms. He tried to go back to his books—the Bar Exam was only weeks away—but try as he might, he couldn't concentrate.

He kept losing himself in dreams that would probably never come true.

## Chapter Fifteen

Elaine had been right in saying that what was needed was time, Holly reflected as she stepped onto the department-store escalator. She was munching on caramel-covered popcorn and peanuts—her third box that day—and she frowned as she emptied the last of it into the palm of one hand. The minute the morning sickness had passed away, the strange cravings had begun. And caramel corn wasn't the only thing she felt compelled to gorge on, unfortunately. Sometimes she wanted smoked oysters rolled in peanut butter....

Holly made a face and then thumped the box against her hand so that the prize would fall out. It was in a white packet, whatever it was, and she tore the paper away as she strolled toward Cookware, where she would teach her last class.

It was an omen! The prize turned out to be an enormous ring with a plastic solitare. Grinning, Holly tucked it into her pocket.

Tonight's project was wonton soup, and the members of her class were at their tables, sleeves rolled up. She scanned their faces as she did every night, hoping to see David among them and, paradoxically, hoping not to.

David had not called her or put in an appearance at her house since the morning he had brought Toby home. Even then, he'd only said that the little boy was worried about being shunted aside when the baby came. And the word "baby" had been like a barrier between them, impossible to surmount.

Holly was saddened as she dropped her caramel corn box surreptitiously into a wastebasket and shrugged out of her coat. Determinedly, she smiled at her students. "Looks like everyone is ready to start."

There were nods, grins and expressions of nervousness all around. And then they began.

It was just as the class was ending that David appeared, his hands wedged into the pockets of a windbreaker emblazoned with the Gonzaga University logo, his eyes carefully avoiding Holly's gaze.

She felt a shivering sort of exhilaration, followed by plunging doubts. Just because David was there, well, that didn't mean that he was ready to make any sort of declaration or renew their relationship. He might even have come to say good-bye, having decided to return to Washington....

This was a considerate class. Each and every student cleaned up his or her own mess, leaving nothing for Holly to do but sneak the occasional glance at David, who was leaning against a refrigerator door, hi arms folded, his navy blue eyes touching upon every-thing except Holly herself.

She smiled as the last good-byes were said and her students departed, certificates in hand. And then she was alone. With David.

"Time to take the bull by the horns, kid," she told herself, drawing on all her courage as she plunged a hand into her coat pocket. Win, lose or draw, there could be no more guesswork and no more emotional sparring. If David Goddard wasn't going to declare himself, then Holly would state her own case and see what happened.

"Hello," she said, walking over to him and stop-ping within touching distance.

David gave her a wry look. Obviously he wasn't going to make this easy.

"Thank you for taking such good care of Toby that night," she said hoarsely. She was clenching her fin-gers so tightly that the small object she held dug into her palm.

"You're welcome," he said.

Holly sighed and rolled her eyes. Now or never, she thought, drawing a deep breath that dizzied her. And then she extended her hand, the plastic ring lying in her palm.

"Will you marry me, David?" she choked out.

He looked as though she had flung wonton soup all over him. His face contorted for a moment and he no longer leaned so indolently against the door of that display-floor refrigerator. No, David stood erect now, Secret-Service alert. His throat worked, but he said nothing.

Holly wanted to die. "You haven't mentioned getting married lately, so I thought I'd bring it up," she said lamely.

Suddenly, so suddenly that Holly jumped, David pulled her against his hard chest, that chest she had so missed the scent and feel and strength of, and he laughed. His hands touched her shoulders briefly and then entwined themselves in her hair, mussing it.

"God, Holly, how I love you," he muttered.

"Does that mean you're going to accept my proposal?" she asked softly, searching his face with wide, cautious eyes.

"How could I refuse?" he asked gruffly, his breath warm against her face, his eyes meeting hers with a direct sort of tenderness that made her shiver with the love of him, the need of him. "Holly, are you sure? Have you thought about this?"

"Yes. To the detriment, I might add, of everything I was supposed to be thinking about instead."

"What made you decide?"

"I didn't need to decide because I already knew. I just needed to *know* I knew."

David rolled his eyes—they were shining with laughter—and then he kissed her. Salespeople and customers were probably looking on, but Holly didn't care. She kissed him back.

She was breathless, moments later, as she caught his hand in hers and tried to wedge the caramel-corn diamond onto his finger. It didn't fit, of course, but David accommodatingly wore it on his pinkie.

"I wonder if accepting an expensive gift like this," David teased, "obligates me to submit to lewd and improper demands."

Holly laughed. "You bet it does," she answered. "Your place or mine, handsome?"

"What about Toby?" he asked, so seriously that Holly's already fathomless love deepened with a painful jolt.

"Toby is spending the night with a friend."

A grin broke over David's wonderful, magnificent face. "You planned this!"

Holly laughed. "Do you really have a hot tub in your bedroom?" she asked. "Rumor has it that you do."

His hand fitted itself to the small of her back and Holly found herself being propeled through Cookware and onto the down escalator. "Rumor is entirely correct," he answered. "All the same, I think you should confirm it with your own eyes."

The hot tub made a lulling, bubbling sound in the semi-darkness, filling the room with a tropical sort of heat. Holly luxuriated in contentment as David's hands slowly divested her of her clothes, pausing now and then to stroke and caress whatever prize he had just uncovered.

"I love you," he said, bending his head to one breast and circling the instantly responsive nipple with the tip of his tongue.

Holly groaned and then, somehow, found the strength to push him away. "Oh, no, you don't, fella. You're not going to stand there in all your clothes and make me crazy."

A compliant sort, David was soon standing there without his clothes. And making her crazy.

She went to stand beside the hot tub, looking down into its churning depths. Then David was behind her, drawing her back against him, running his hands from her waist to her breasts. He seemed to be weighing them in his palms, and Holly moaned and let her head fall back against his shoulder as his thumbs coaxed her nipples to a new level of response.

When Holly thought she could bear no more of that, when she was sure she would have to turn to him and demand that he take her, he retraced his path, lingering at her hips for a delicious moment and then knitting his fingers together over her abdomen.

His teeth caught at her earlobe and she quivered against the sinewy length of him, the hair on his chest tickling her naked back. "I want this to last forever," he breathed and again she trembled. "Cold?" he queried as an afterthought.

"Hardly," Holly managed to say.

All the same, David lowered her gently into the hot tub. The warm, moving water seemed to intensify the raging need in her senses to an almost unbearable degree, but Holly hadn't the strength to lift herself out.

Kneeling behind her, David took her hands in his and positioned them so that they were cupped behind her head. And then he began, idly, to toy with her breasts again, now bathing them with warm water, now caressing them, now plying the nipples between skilled fingers. Holly moaned and her own fingers uncurled, but she did not try to lower her arms.

"David," she finally managed to say, "oh, David— make love to me—now—"

He drew her up out of the water and placed her on the tiled edge. Even in the half-darkness, she could see the glittering hunger in his eyes, a hunger he appeased at her breasts until Holly was writhing with need, her body still slick and warm from the brief episode in the hot tub.

"I—"

"David," Holly tangled her hands in his thick, dark, rumpled hair. "Now."

"I might hurt you—the baby—"

The concern in his voice caused Holly to free her hands and capture his muscle-corded thighs instead, urging him toward her. "I need you, David. I love you. And we've already waited long enough."

With a moan, he lowered himself to her and sought her solace with his manhood. His welcome was such that, with a rasped exclamation, he surged inside her, deeply but gently. Holly drew her knees up and felt his powerful hips moving slowly against her inner thighs.

She watched him until she could no longer bear the shadowy beauty of him and then closed her eyes. Patches of golden light exploded behind her lids as new feelings blossomed within her like flowers.

David, in turn, was nearly incoherent. "I thought this—would never—happen again—oh, God, Holly—how I need you—"

Holly muttered some wicked sweetness and her reward was a breathtaking increase in the pace of their lovemaking. Their bodies rose and fell in fierce unison, fever after fever raging within Holly and then breaking, each one making her wilder. Her fingernails raked David's back, as his possession and her own became one and the same and they both cried out as the tender anguish bonded them, fusing them into one being with its heat.

David collapsed beside her, his body trembling, his breath a primitive, tearing sound. "Good Lord, woman," he managed after some time, "I'm not sure I can bear up under a lifetime of that."

Holly stretched languidly, an evil wanton in the warm, lush darkness. "You'll 'bear up' just fine," she said, winding a finger in the moist down curling upon his chest.

He laughed, turned her onto her side and gave her bottom a playful swat. "Vamp," he said. "Just for that, I think I'll carry you to my bed and prove your theory."

"You couldn't carry me if you had to," challenged Holly in a sensuous, stretching purr. "Your knees are too weak."

"Is that so?" he asked in a rumbling whisper. And then, as Holly had hoped, he rolled to his feet, pulled her after him and lifted her into his arms. Feigning a dark passion, he dropped her from shoulder height onto the bed, which received her gently, swaying and undulating under her weight.

"Ummm," Holly crooned, stretching her arms upward. David fell to her, setting the waves inside the mattress in frantic motion again, a motion that never really stopped throughout that long, glorious night.

## EPILOGUE

Holly Goddard glared at her computer screen, muttering. This book had started out as a mystery, and her agent had liked what she had seen of it, but now it seemed to be taking an unexpected direction.

"It's Saturday," Holly grumbled to herself. "In some religions, Saturday is a day of rest."

"Did you say something?" David asked from the doorway of the study they shared. He was wearing blue jeans, a maroon sweat shirt, a denim jacket—and a baby girl in the carrier on his back.

Born in late September, Miss Autumn Goddard was already spending most Saturdays in the park with David and Toby. Her cheeks were pink and her round, indigo eyes sleepy as they peered out of the tiny snowsuit she wore.

Holly was filled with such tenderness that she ached. She forgot the problems she was having with her novel and went to plant a kiss on Autumn's plump cheek before lifting her out of the carrier to cuddle her for a moment.

"Where's Toby?" she asked.

David grinned, sliding back the hood of Autumn's snowsuit, revealing a head of curly, Holly-gold hair. He kissed the baby's forehead briefly before answering, "Downstairs, doing his homework with Marcus."

Marcus was Toby's newest and "bestest" friend; since he and Holly had moved into David's condo, the very day of the wedding, the two little boys had been a package deal. If you wanted one, you had to accept the other.

"Don't you have any homework to do, counselor?" Holly teased as she carried Autumn into the bedroom that adjoined her own and David's. "You have a big case coming up this week, if I remember correctly."

David dodged the question by disappearing into the kitchen, but he was back soon enough, Autumn's naptime bottle in hand.

Holly had already undressed their daughter, changed her diaper and bundled her into a cuddly pink sleeper. Autumn extended her tiny hands at the sight of the offered bottle and was asleep after a few gurgling swallows.

"About your case," Holly prodded, in the living room. Dammit, if she had to work on Saturday, then David was going to be right there in the study with her, plugging away at *Snider vs McCulley*.

Showing not the slightest sign of industry, David sat down on the raised hearth of the fireplace and stared indolently down at his right sneaker, his chin resting on one knee. "I've got that case down pat and you know it."

"Is that so?"

"Yes," David replied flatly, his eyes sparkling as they met hers. "You have to work so you want me to suffer right along beside you—misery loves company and all that."

"I'll be misery and you be company," Holly grumbled, assessing the situation. Toby was downstairs, visiting Marcus. Autumn was asleep. She blushed at the course her thoughts were taking.

David grinned. "And you'll love me?" he leered.

"Any time I get the chance," Holly admitted.

He assumed his best attorney manner, frowning pensively, standing up to pace back and forth along the hearth as though it were a jury box. "What about your book, Mrs. Goddard?" he demanded soberly. "How do you intend to meet your deadline if you don't write?"

Holly shrugged, her legs curled beneath her on the navy blue sofa. "I made up the deadline myself. There's no reason to be picky, here."

"Picky?" David boomed, looking suitably shocked, even horrified. He shook his head as he continued to pace, his hands locked behind his back. "Have you no dedication, Mrs. Goddard? No ambition? No—"

Holly giggled at the picture he made. "Don't tease me, David," she wailed. "My plot is so hopelessly snarled that I'll never get it undone and my characters won't do anything I tell them to!"

David stopped, bending slightly to peer into Holly's face. "Exactly what kind of scene are you trying to write, anyway?" he demanded in that same ponderous, lawyerlike tone.

Holly gave him a once-over from beneath coyly lowered eyelashes. "A love scene, of course," she purred.

"Aha!" he cried, pointing one index finger into the air. "In that case, madam we are able to ascertain the exact nature of your problem!"

Holly pretended to peer around him. "We?" she echoed.

"Speaking as the prosecution, of course," he admitted.

"Of course. And what, pray tell, is the 'exact nature of my problem,' counselor?"

"Research, of course. A pitiable, contemptible lack of research."

"I see," Holly said, assuming a look of deep chagrin.

"No, Madam," David went on sternly, "I don't think you do see. This is a matter of the gravest importance."

Holly giggled again. "You don't really say things like that in the courtroom, do you?"

"No," David confessed. "I saw it in an old Henry Fonda movie. Now, exactly how do you plead? Guilty or not guilty?"

Holly deliberately batted her eyelashes. "Of what am I accused, sir?"

He sank to his knees before her with a comical thump, his eyes gleaming. "Neglecting your research," he replied.

Thinking of the weeks after Autumn's birth when there had been no lovemaking at all, and the hesitant quality in David's touch even now, Holly's playful mood was dampened. "Or perhaps of neglecting my husband?" she prompted softly.

He bent forward and kissed her. "Never that," he whispered.

"I know it was hard for you—"

David laid an index finger to her lips. "Having a baby was no piece of cake, either, I'll wager. Still, Autumn is almost two months old. Time is passing us by. Maybe we should start another baby right away."

Holly laughed and wrapped her arms around his neck. "I love you, you maniac."

"And I love you. But, as a writer, that doesn't excuse you from doing proper research." He stood up, drawing Holly with him, pulling her against the appealing, granitelike length of him. His face was serious, though, despite his earlier teasing. "Tell me the truth. Does it...does it hurt when I make love to you?"

She stood up on tiptoe to kiss his chin. "No. It feels glorious."

"Really?"

"Would I lie about something as important as research?" She slid her arms around his waist and felt him tremble as their bodies touched, her soft curves a temptation to his hard lines and angles.

"I certainly hope not," he gasped, gazing deep into her eyes, finding things she might have hidden once but was willing to share now. His hands came tentatively to burrow into her silky hair. "Oh, Holly," he breathed. "Holly. Every day, I wake up and I think I can't possibly love you any more than I already do. And every day, you prove me wrong."

Holly's eyes misted with happy tears. "Do you love me enough to help me with my research?" she whispered.

David laughed and swatted her firm, round bottom with both hands. "Oh, at least that much. I'm in the mood to be magnanimous here."

Holly gave him a long look. "Then what's holding you back? Carry me off to your bed and slake your savage passion at my heaving breasts."

David grinned and feigned a beleaguered look. "God, I hope that isn't a direct quote from your manuscript, woman," he teased. "If it is, you'd better go back to writing about crumpets and wontons."

Holly wriggled against him in reply, and he groaned, lifting her into his arms. "If we're going to research savage passion, I guess we'd better get started."

Their passion was not savage, but tender, mounting with every kiss, every caress, every surrender of a garment. Though they had made love several times since Autumn's birth, David was still afraid of hurting her.

As Holly lay beneath him, her blouse and bra gone, her breasts proudly bared to him, David bent his head and kissed each impudent peak. "Allow me, Madam," he taunted in a rumbling voice, "to slake my savage something or other."

The kisses felt so good that Holly stretched, crooning and thrusting herself upward for more. "Please, do," she said and she whimpered with pleasure as he began to lose his restraint and enjoy her freely, now nibbling, now suckling with the fierce hunger Holly craved.

Finally, leaving breasts moistened and tuned to passion by his lips and his tongue, David traced a path of kisses over her collarbone and up her neck to the sensitive hollows beneath her ears.

"Are you taking notes?" he demanded, working his way back down to a breast, attending to it briefly, and then moving on to the heaving ridges of her rib cage.

"C-Copious notes," Holly choked as he circled her navel with a leisure that was positively torturous. She moaned with sweet despondency as his kisses continued. "Th-that isn't at all p-pertinent to my wo-work, sir."

He chuckled, the sound far away and yet so near as to be a part of Holly. "Want to bet?" he asked, his hand stroking her inner thigh, pressing her legs to part.

Research was the furthest thing from Holy's mind then—moments later, she didn't even have a mind, for she had been driven out of it. Only later, after a series of shattering releases, after David had finally given in to her pleading and entered her, his body at once taming and exalting hers, was she free to grope her way back toward sanity.

He lay beside her afterward, his head pillowed on her breasts, his legs still entangled with hers. Smiling to herself, Holly wound a lock of his hair around her finger and speculated, "I think I've got it. I know what I was doing wrong now."

"Believe me," David rasped, still too weak, apparently, to rise from her breast, "you didn't do anything wrong."

Holly laughed. "I was talking about my book, silly."

David growled with pretended outrage and rolled onto his back, hauling Holly up to sit astride him. It was so good, this easiness between them, this lack of restraint or caution. Tears of sheer joy blurred Holly's vision.

David frowned and caught them on his thumbs when they fell. "What is it, love?"

Holly was anxious to reassure him, and she gave a sniffling laugh. "I'm afraid I've used you shamelessly," she confessed.

"How so?"

"I'm not writing a romance; I'm writing a mystery. The love scene I was talking about consists of one kiss, nothing more."

David glared at her, pretending outraged honor. "Wench," he said in gravelly tones, "you'll have to pay for that."

"I will?" Holly questioned, the picture of innocence. "How?"

He shifted slightly and then entered her with an authority that made her gasp with pleasure. His hands rose with brazen idleness to cup her breasts. And that was answer enough.

Holly began to move upon him, slowly, sweetly, a creature of fire and instinct. "You are completely— oh, God—without conscience—"

David matched her pace and then began to set one of his own. "Completely," he agreed, pressing his head back into the pillows and closing his eyes. Several glorious, heated minutes passed, and then they were both crying out for each other, even though they were already joined, seeking each other with desperate hands and hoarse, tender words.

The finding was sweet indeed.

Turkeys. David's fancy refrigerator, with its sliding opaque door, was covered with construction-paper turkeys. Holding a fussy Autumn against her hip with one arm, Holly opened the appliance's door with the other and reached inside for milk.

The draperies had not been drawn, and as Holly sat at the table, rocking her hungry daughter in her arms while the bottle heated, she looked out over the sparkling lights of the city, thinking.

Impatient for her midnight feeding, Autumn flung back her gossamer-tufted head and wailed.

"Shhh," Holly whispered against a tiny neck scented of talcum powder and baby lotion. "You'll wake up Daddy and Toby."

Autumn was unimpressed with that possibility. Her wail intensified to a series of piercing shrieks. Chuckling softly, Holly took the bottle from its warmer and did the gyrations required to hold a furious baby and test the heat of the milk at the same time.

"This looks like a job for Super-lawyer," yawned David, clad in a velour bathrobe, as he took both baby and bottle from Holly and plopped down in a chair. A moment later, Autumn was imbibing greedily.

"Fine thing," Holly scoffed with mock indignation. "I do all the work and you get the credit."

David only grinned, watching his daughter with such adoration in his eyes that Holly wasn't sure she could bear it. Or the feelings inspired in her.

"There was a letter from Craig today," she said quietly, leaning back against the counter, her arms folded. She felt like a housewifely bundle of chenille and love.

David's eyes darted to her face, wary. "Oh? How is he?"

"He's getting better," Holly answered gently. "They haven't decided yet exactly what to try him for. It might be a long time before they do."

There was a silence; obviously David didn't know what to say. And Holly didn't want Craig or anyone else to stand between them.

She went to David and made a place for herself on his knee, unsettling the ravenous Autumn only slightly. Wrapping one arm around David's neck, Holly intoned, "Kiss me, you fool!"

He laughed and responded accordingly.

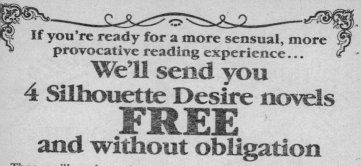

If you're ready for a more sensual, more provocative reading experience...

# We'll send you
# 4 Silhouette Desire novels
# FREE
## and without obligation

Then, we'll send you six more Silhouette Desire® novels to preview every month for 15 days with absolutely no obligation!

When you decide to keep them, you pay just $1.95 each ($2.25 each in Canada) *with never any additional charges!*

And that's not all. You get FREE home delivery of all books as soon as they are published and a FREE subscription to the Silhouette Books Newsletter as long as you remain a member. Each issue is filled with news on upcoming titles, interviews with your favorite authors, even their favorite recipes.

Silhouette Desire novels are not for everyone. They are written especially for the woman who wants a more satisfying, more deeply involving reading experience. Silhouette Desire novels take you *beyond* the others.

If you're ready for that kind of experience, fill out and return the coupon today!

## Silhouette ❦ Desire®

**Silhouette Books, 120 Brighton Rd., P.O. Box 5084, Clifton, NJ 07015-5084**

---

### Clip and mail to: Silhouette Books,
### 120 Brighton Road, P.O. Box 5084, Clifton, NJ 07015-5084

**YES.** Please send me 4 FREE Silhouette Desire novels. Unless you hear from me after I receive them, send me 6 new Silhouette Desire novels to preview each month as soon as they are published. I understand you will bill me just $1.95 each, a total of $11.70 (in Canada, $2.25 each, a total of $13.50)—with no additional shipping, handling, or other charges of any kind. There is no minimum number of books that I must buy, and I can cancel at any time. The first 4 books are mine to keep.                    **BD18R6**

Name _____ (please print)

Address _____ Apt. #

City _____ State/Prov. _____ Zip/Postal Code

* In Canada, mail to: Silhouette Canadian Book Club, 320 Steelcase Rd., E., Markham, Ontario, L3R 2M1, Canada
Terms and prices subject to change.
SILHOUETTE DESIRE is a service mark and registered trademark.        D-SUB-1

# *Silhouette Special Edition*

## COMING NEXT MONTH

**RETURN TO PARADISE—Jennifer West**
Reeve Ferris was swiftly rising to stardom, yet he couldn't forget
Jamie Quinn, the small-town girl who had captured his heart along
the way.

**REFLECTIONS OF YESTERDAY—Debbie Macomber**
Angie knew the minute she saw Simon that twelve years had
changed nothing; she was still destined to love him, and they still
seemed destined to be kept apart.

**VEIN OF GOLD—Elaine Camp**
Houston had the land, and Faith had the skill. They were an unlikely
team, but side by side they drilled the Texas soil for oil and found
riches within each other.

**SUMMER WINE—Freda Vasilos**
The romance of Greece drew Sara into Nick's arms, but when the
spell was broken she knew she could never leave her life in Boston
for this alluring man . . . or could she?

**DREAM GIRL—Tracy Sinclair**
For an internationally known model like Angelique Archer, having a
secret admirer was not that unusual, but finding out he was royalty
was definitely not an everyday occurrence!

**SECOND NATURE—Nora Roberts**
Lenore was the first reporter to get the opportunity to interview best-
selling author Hunter Brown. On a camping trip in Arizona she
learned more about Hunter and herself than she'd bargained for.

---

## AVAILABLE NOW:

**STATE SECRETS**
Linda Lael Miller

**DATELINE: WASHINGTON**
Patti Beckman

**ASHES OF THE PAST**
Monica Barrie

**STRING OF PEARLS**
Natalie Bishop

**LOVE'S PERFECT ISLAND**
Rebecca Swan

**DEVIL'S GAMBIT**
Lisa Jackson